AUS

Melody Cameron finds a happiness she had never dreamed of when she takes on a private nursing assignment near the beautiful Austrian city of Salzburg. But can her feelings for Dr Dieter von Rheinhof bring her anything more than heartache?

*Books you will enjoy
in our Doctor–Nurse series*

FIRST-YEAR'S FANCY by Lynne Collins
DESERT FLOWER by Dana James
INDIAN OCEAN DOCTORS by Juliet Shore
CRUISE NURSE by Clare Lavenham
CAPTIVE HEART by Hazel Fisher
A PROFESSIONAL SECRET by Kate Norway
NURSE ON CALL by Leonie Craig
THE GILDED CAGE by Sarah Franklin
A SURGEON CALLED AMANDA by Elizabeth Harrison
VICTORY FOR VICTORIA by Betty Neels
SHAMROCK NURSE by Elspeth O'Brien
ICE VENTURE NURSE by Lydia Balmain
TREAD SOFTLY, NURSE by Lynne Collins
DR VENABLES' PRACTICE by Anne Vinton
NURSE OVERBOARD by Meg Wisgate
EMERGENCY NURSE by Grace Read
DOCTORS IN DISPUTE by Jean Evans
WRONG DOCTOR JOHN by Kate Starr
SECOND CHANCE AT LOVE by Zara Holman
TRIO OF DOCTORS by Lindsay Hicks
CASSANDRA BY CHANCE by Betty Neels

AUSTRIAN INTERLUDE

BY
LEE STAFFORD

MILLS & BOON LIMITED
London · Sydney · Toronto

First published in Great Britain 1983
by Mills & Boon Limited, 15–16 Brook's Mews,
London WlA lDR

© Lee Stafford 1983

Australian copyright 1983
Philippine copyright 1983

ISBN 0 263 74406 X

Set in 10 on 11½ pt Linotron Times
03/0983–75,000

Photoset by Rowland Phototypesetting Ltd
Bury St Edmunds, Suffolk
Made and printed in Great Britain by
Richard Clay (The Chaucer Press) Ltd
Bungay, Suffolk

CHAPTER ONE

SHE noticed the man the moment she took her seat on the plane. Almost before she had strapped herself in, and felt the motion of the engine as the aircraft taxied down the runway, gathering momentum and straining towards the final unleashing of energy that would render them airborne.

It would have been difficult not to notice him, Melody thought reluctantly, for he was of a striking and distinctive appearance. His was one of those young-old faces, attractively creased, to which it was almost impossible to put a definite age, the closest guess she could make was somewhere in his thirties. He had a fine head of shining, vigorously brushed hair, which reminded her of a field of ripened wheat, springing back from an ascetic forehead, and he was tall—this she could ascertain from the relaxed length of leg stretched out, and the hands that lay along the arms of the seat were slim, with long, tapering fingers.

But what really held her attention as the aircraft cleaved through the layer of cloud into the untroubled blue of evening above, was the fact that his eyes were closed, his face and his whole body were in an enviable state of repose. Obviously, since they had just boarded the plane, he was not asleep, besides which, although tranquil, there was a sense of awareness about him. It was as if, although present, he was suspended in a different continuum of existence, and Melody gazed at him fascinated, although she knew it was rude to stare.

The eyelids flickered, he opened his eyes, and quickly she looked away, but not before she observed that they were the blue-grey of a rainwashed sky. They were also very penetrating, and she did not particularly welcome anyone looking behind the carefully assumed calm of her own face, not right now. She knew he had caught her watching him, and the brief silence which ensued was embarrassing for Melody, who busied herself unfastening her seat belt and rearranging her handbag and magazines, hoping the moment would pass unremarked.

But it was too much for her to expect that her discomfiture would remain unnoticed, and her companion shifted his long frame in his seat, half turning towards her. There was just a touch of amusement in his voice, a hint of condescension, as if he felt a moral obligation to reassure this silly girl at his side, as he said,

'There is no need for you to be alarmed, or fear that I am about to suffer some kind of seizure, *fraulein*. I was merely meditating.'

The last thing, the very last thing Melody needed was to get into casual conversation with a man. That way trouble lay, and grief, and guilt, and all the reasons why she was now sitting on a plane, heading into the unknown, instead of safely back in the only real home she had ever known, with a secure job and prospects of promotion assuring her future. But he had spoken to her, and it was impossible for her to avoid answering.

'M—meditating?' she repeated, uncomfortably aware that her own voice sounded hesitant and slightly stupid. 'You mean you were in a trance?'

'Not at all,' he contradicted, with a kind of lofty patience. 'Meditation is simply a technique of deep breathing and controlled thought, long practised in the

East, and known to all disciples of yoga, which induces relaxation.'

'I see,' said Melody, feeling small. Nervousness caused her to rush on, 'It certainly seems to work. This is my first flight, and I was feeling very jittery, but you were amazingly relaxed.'

'It works,' he said calmly. 'I don't care very much for flying, but since I necessarily have to do quite a lot of it, I would be foolish not to evolve some method of coping with the stress.'

He looked so serene and in command of himself that Melody could not imagine him ever being a prey to fear or uncertainty. Her own hands were still trembling from the build up of tension before take-off, and she gave a small, nervous laugh, saying ruefully,

'I wish you would explain to me how to achieve this enviable state.'

His smile was polite, but distant, letting her know in no uncertain terms that this conversation had gone as far as he wished it to.

'I imagine there are classes for such things,' he said, with an air of dismissal.

Melody subsided, snubbed. He had made it plain that he did not want to involve himself in any further con- versation with her, and really, she should not object to this, she thought, reminding herself of the inner pledge she had made. NO MEN was her prime commandment, and the fact that she was sitting next to an attractive and fascinating stranger on a plane should not cause her to make an exception to this self-imposed rule. She told herself that her desire to talk had stemmed only from nerves, because she was alone and not a little apprehen- sive of the step she was taking, and if he considered himself above exchanging casual pleasantries with an unknown and insignificant girl, well, that was fine with her.

The air stewardess was coming down the aisle with her trolley, dispensing drinks. He ordered a whisky and soda for himself, and with the same formal correctness, turned to Melody and asked,

'Would you care for a drink? Coffee?'

'No thank you,' she said primly, still stinging from his earlier put-down, and anxious to salvage her own pride. 'I think I'll just read my magazines, if you don't mind.'

'Not in the least,' he said coolly, and taking a sheaf of typewritten papers from his briefcase, began to study them so intently that Melody believed he was soon unaware of her presence. If he were piqued, it was only for a moment. He was an extremely attractive and distinguished-looking man, most likely a business executive of some kind, successful, no doubt, and well off, if the cut of his clothes were anything to judge by. Why should he be even mildly interested in her? If they had not happened to be seated next to one another, he most probably would not have given her a second glance.

She did not fully understand why, but his calm indifference filled her with a fresh and painful realisation of her utter aloneness, which made her blink back threatened tears.

Pull yourself together, Melody, she urged herself. She had always been alone. It was just that before there was the enveloping security of ordered hospital routine, its continuity unvarying from day to day, beneath whatever temporary crisis was occurring. It had been her life, as student and qualified SRN for several years, and since she was an orphan and had spent most of her youth in various institutions, it had come to represent home and family to her. Now it was gone.

She would do well to remember that, she reflected, if she were ever again tempted, as she had been a few moments ago, to believe that no possible harm could ensue from talking to a man, from offering friendship and understanding. She had done that once before, and the result had been that awful morning she would never forget, when she had walked, in unknowing innocence, into the ward, to be greeted by a shocked silence. And the only person who would tell her what had happened was the new student nurse, who waded in, in ignorance, where others feared to tread.

'Haven't you heard? The whole hospital is talking about it.' The girl's eyes were wide with a kind of fascinated horror.

'Heard what? I've come straight on duty from the nurses' home, and haven't even had the radio on,' Melody had joked. 'Has World War III started, or something?'

'No! It's James Garret, the hospital administrator, and his wife. A car accident. She drove it straight into a wall they reckon. Both of them were killed outright.'

Melody had simply stood, whilst the floors echoed with the busy feet of staff going about their work, staring ahead of her like a zombie. She was dimly aware of Sister coming up, taking her arm and giving her a slight shake. 'Come on, Nurse. Best to keep busy, and goodness knows, we've enough to do.'

But she could not take it in. James and Liane, dead. Both of them. She drove it into a wall – been drinking, they say. Someone heard them arguing in the social club, but you know how it was. Snippets of gossip filtered through to her during the day, overheard from little enclaves which dispersed or fell silent at her approach. She did not understand this conspiracy not to talk about the tragedy in her presence – after all, they had been her friends, and she could not pretend it hadn't happened.

Actually, it had been Liane she befriended first, when she arrived with her husband who was taking up his new post as hospital administrator. Coming off duty one day, she had spotted the young woman in the car park, trying vainly to get her car started.

Liane, blonde hair in an attractively dishevelled tumble about her lovely face, eyes bright, had smiled ruefully at her out of the car window.

'Know anything about cars?' she called.

Melody paused.

'Enough to drive one myself, but I'm no mechanical wizard,' she confessed. 'What seems to be the matter?'

'Not a clue,' the other replied insouciantly. 'I called in to see James in his office, but he was at a meeting, and now this damn thing won't start.'

Coming closer, Melody's trained, observant eye was swift to observe the flushed brightness of Liane Garret's face, the frenzied aimlessness of her demeanour.

'Move over and let me have a try,' she suggested, and slid into the driving seat. There was an unmistakable smell of spirits in the car. Young Mrs Garret had clearly been drinking, and quite heavily. Melody turned the key in the ignition, and, after a couple of tries, the engine responded readily enough.

'It's all right. I think you had simply stalled it, and hadn't waited long enough before trying again,' she said.

'Patience isn't one of my virtues,' admitted Liane with a grin. She was not obviously drunk, her words were not slurred, and her manner, although excitable, could have been simply the natural exuberance of an extrovert personality, but Melody was not fooled.

'I think I had better drive you home,' she said, and Liane seemed to collapse all at once.

'Yes. Perhaps you had,' she said, and lapsed into silence, apart from monosyllabic directions, which was unnerving after her erstwhile brightness.

The Garret home was a modern detached house in one of the newer suburbs, and Melody found herself making coffee in the smart, melamine-surfaced kitchen, whilst Liane languished on the sofa in the lounge. But after several cups of coffee she became lively and talkative once more, and regaled Melody with the story of what she called the sad existence of a neglected hospital admin. wife, marooned in a strange town where she knew no one, whilst her husband worked excessively long hours and came home terse and exhausted.

Melody was still there when James Garret arrived home, and it was largely thanks to her that there was dinner to put on the table for him.

'This is Melody, my new friend and guardian angel,' Liane told him expansively, and in his tired eyes, Melody read all too plainly that he was aware of how his wife spent a good deal of her time.

In the months that followed Melody saw a lot of the Garrets. She spent much of her free time with Liane, for whom she felt a deep, instinctive sympathy. The young woman was cut off from her family background, and Melody, who had never known a family at all, could imagine what it must be like to have this support pulled from under one.

Liane was a delightful and entertaining companion when she was in the mood to be. But she could just as easily be sunk in the depths of depression, and these two states alternated wildly. Depressed and lethargic, or frenetically bright and active, she tended to turn to alcohol as a stimulant or as a sedative. She did not believe she needed medical help with her problems. Okay, she was a bit moody, so what, and she liked a drink, but did that make her an alcoholic? It seemed all Melody could give her was steadfast friendship, and she gave that willingly enough. What Liane craved was attention, and however much she got, it would never be sufficient.

Melody could not pinpoint exactly the time James began to seek her out as a confidante. To begin with, he used to waylay her in the canteen and tell her his worries about Liane. She was drinking too much but would not seek advice. He worried about her being alone all day, about her driving the car in an unfit state. And she would not understand that he had his job to do—to her, that was a rival she must conquer, or destroy herself in the attempt.

Once or twice he took Melody to lunch, simply to unburden himself. And then he was no longer talking only about Liane, but about his job, and the problems connected with it, which he was unable to discuss with his wife.

'You're easy to talk to, Melody,' he told her, more than once. 'I can't see why some man hasn't snapped you up yet.'

She laughed.

'When he does, I'll let you have the privilege of giving me away,' she said. And that was precisely how she saw him, not as a father, he was much too young, but as an elder brother, for whom she had respect and concern. It did not occur to her—perhaps it should have—that others saw them together and formed conclusions that were less than charitable. Garret's wife was unstable and drank, so he had found himself a pretty little nurse, and who could blame him?

'I thought you were my friend!' Liane cried accusingly one afternoon, when Melody found her sprawled on the sofa with the remains of a bottle of whisky on the table before her. And even that did not penetrate her innocence.

'I am your friend,' she returned equably, confiscating the bottle and opening the windows.

'Not everyone thinks so,' Liane rejoined.

Melody took the empty glass into the kitchen and returned with a cloth to wipe the table. She was about to ask Liane what she meant by that, but the other girl had fallen into a heavy, stupefied sleep, and remained so for the rest of the afternoon. Melody left as James arrived home.

'Liane's asleep—don't wake her,' she whispered.

He pressed her fingers briefly between his.

'Good girl,' he said gratefully, and she slipped quietly out. That was the last time she saw either of them.

At the inquest, the coroner recorded a verdict of death by misadventure. But the verdict of hospital gossip had it otherwise, and it was not long before this version began to filter through to Melody, still shocked by the tragic death of her friends. At the very least, she discovered appalled, many believed that she and James had been having an affair, that Liane knew, and that this was the cause of the quarrel in the social club on the night of the accident. Worse, there was a rumour circulating that it had not been an accident at all, but a kind of suicide, that Liane had deliberately crashed the car, killing herself and her husband, in protest against his infidelity. After all, everyone knew she was unstable.

Melody knew who was responsible for starting this story on its rounds. When the job on Orthopaedics had come up and she had applied for it, Nurse Laura Bailey had also wanted the appointment, and had been bitterly aggrieved by her failure. Ever since, Melody had been conscious of a carefully veiled resentment on the other girl's part, but it had been an unpleasant experience, nonetheless, to walk into the nurses' rest-room one day and overhear Laura Bailey expounding this theory to a small group of spellbound listeners.

What she should have done, Melody realised later, was confront her there and then, and ask her to repeat what she had said to her face, then refute it strongly. But she was still sickened by the whole business, and even to contemplate it made her feel physically ill. So she simply turned and walked out, aware that by doing so she had more or less admitted her guilt.

And it hit her like a thunderbolt, as she ran along corridors where no nurse was permitted to run, and out, gasping, into the fresh air. What if it were, at least in essence, true? What if Liane *had* believed it, and had deliberately smashed herself and James into oblivion as a result? That, more than the malicious gossip or the sidelong glances, was what haunted her nights, and made her days impossible.

It was clear to Melody that she could no longer remain working at the hospital where she had been so content hitherto, where now curious and sometimes hostile glances followed her wherever she went, and even her friends were strangely silent in her company. Nor could she live in the small country town she had made her home, for in such a close community, where everyone knew everyone else, it would take a long time to live down the rumours. She offered her resignation, which was accepted without demur. Even Matron realised that Melody was in an impossible situation.

But she stayed and worked out her full month's notice, refusing to run away from the increasingly hostile whispers and glances. As the month drew to its close, she had still done nothing about applying for another job in a different part of the country. It was as if any hospital, anywhere, would remind her of what had happened here, and she would never be free of the lingering aura of guilt.

Melody had no family to turn to, to support her through this difficult time. Emotionally and financially, she was on her own, and she realised she would have to get a job of some kind to support herself. Also, with the termination of her service, she would have to vacate her room in the nurses' home, and find herself somewhere else to live. The time was getting perilously short, and soon, if she did not rouse herself from the inertia which seemed to have her in its grip, she would quite literally be out on the streets with no means of support.

Help came at the last minute, from a totally unexpected quarter. A week before she was due to leave, Melody was in the canteen, taking a solitary lunch break, when a kindly voice said,

'I was told I would find you here. Do you mind if I join you with my coffee?'

Melody looked up, surprised to see Mrs Moore, the president of the hospital's League of Friends. She knew her slightly, having helped with some of that lady's fund-raising activities, but could not imagine why she should specially seek her out.

'No, of course I don't mind,' she smiled. She was late for her break, the canteen was virtually empty, and the company would make a change from her own gloomy thoughts.

'I heard you were leaving,' Mrs Moore began, and as a

spasm of pain crossed Melody's guileless face, she put a
hand quickly over that of the girl.

'No, my dear, I am not going to ask you a lot of
awkward and quite unwarranted questions. I'm around
here often enough to have heard the rumours, and let me
just say I don't believe a word of them. You're not the
type to be involved with someone else's husband.'

Melody swallowed uncomfortably, a little overcome
by the straightforward kindness of this near-stranger's
belief in her innocence.

'Thank you. I wish everyone agreed with you,' she
said ruefully.

'Oh, some people just like a scandal, and don't particularly care who their gossip hurts. It's human nature
to believe the worst, I'm afraid,' the league president
said dismissively. 'However, to get back to the reason
why I wanted to see you—Sister on your ward speaks
highly of your work, and she tells me that you have
not, as yet, found another position.'

'No.' Melody could not resist the impulse to confide in
this sympathetic woman. 'I haven't really looked for
one. I feel as if I couldn't take any more of hospital life,
after . . . after . . . And yet, nursing is all I am trained
for, and I love it. I'm aware that's something of a
contradiction,' she added lamely.

'Most of life is a contradiction, my dear. But your case
is perfectly understandable. You still want to nurse, but
you feel you would like to get away from the hospital
environment for a while. And I, as luck would have it,
know of a family who would like to employ a nurse on a
private basis. It seems we ought to be able to put the two
together and come up with something.'

Melody's hazel eyes opened very wide, and for the
first time since the tragedy, a flutter of interest stirred in

her, which the other woman was quick to note.

'You would like to know more?'

'Yes, please.'

'Very well. These people have a much loved and indulged only daughter, who suffered a very bad riding accident, with spinal injuries which made them fear that she might be a paraplegic for the rest of her life. But after many months in hospital, and a good partial recovery, she is now being sent home, and medical opinion is that, with time, her chances of a normal life are excellent. It is felt that being in her own home again will aid her recovery. But Kristina is confined to a wheelchair at present, and her mother and stepfather—she is the child of her mother's first marriage—feel that to have a qualified nurse on hand would reassure them greatly, and be of tremendous help to the girl.'

Melody took a long, deep breath.

'They want a nurse to live with them in their home, and help look after . . . Kristina, did you say her name was?'

'Yes. She's nineteen. So a young, but qualified nurse would be a helpful factor psychologically, too. I think you are a compassionate and sensible young person, and Matron is willing to give you a reference attesting to your qualifications and character. You have worked on orthopaedics, too, which is useful. So what do you think, Nurse? Would you like to take the job?'

The rush of hope and gladness in the girl's eyes spoke more than words ever could. Here was a chance to continue nursing, when she had thought all she could do was take a job in a shop or factory. A chance, too, for something she had never known—to live in a family, even though she would only be an employee, and not really part of it.

'I really think I would,' she said. 'How do I go about applying for it? I suppose they—the family—will want to interview me.'

Mrs Moore smiled.

'That would be difficult,' she said. 'I think Matron's recommendation, and my own, would suffice for them to employ you on a trial basis, and from there, you would have to see how you got on. You see, they live near Salzburg. Rather a long way to go for an interview.'

Melody gasped.

'Salzburg? In Austria?' she exclaimed. 'You didn't tell me that before!'

'No, I didn't. I did not think you were the kind of girl to take a job like this merely as an opportunity to live in a very beautiful place, but I wanted to be sure, first, that you were interested in the position for its own sake. Have you been to Austria before?'

Melody was still recovering from her amazement.

'I've never been further than the Isle of Wight!' she said. 'The nearest I've been to Austria is when I saw *The Sound of Music* at the local cinema. It all looked lovely, of course, but Mrs Moore, I don't think I can take this job you've told me about. For a start, I don't speak German very fluently, only the little I learned at school, and . . .'

The older woman did not seem at all perturbed by Melody's reluctance.

'Don't worry. Kristina's father, Eva Schulz's first husband, was English, and the girl was brought up here. That's how I came to know them. The whole family speaks English fluently. Eva's present husband is a very successful architect, and they are quite prosperous, I understand, although I have not seen their home. You'll find them charming. Kristina was a bit of a minx as a

child, but she really has been dreadfully ill, and you will
be able to help her, which is what nursing is all about,
after all.'

Melody had to agree with that last statement one
hundred per cent, and as she assimilated the idea which
had first seemed so alarming, it began to lose its strange-
ness. She began to see it not as a revolutionary notion,
but as something she could quite well do, and then, as
something she would *like* to do.

A change of scene. She had said that was what she
needed, and what could be more of a change? A private
home in Austria after a hospital in a small English town?
And she already felt a genuine sympathy for the injured
girl she had never met. Yes, she would go. And there, in
Austria, she would put the awful memories of the past
weeks behind her, she would concentrate on her work to
the exclusion of everything, she promised herself.

Seated on the plane, reliving all that had led up to this
flight into the unknown, Melody could not resist a covert
glance at the man in the next seat. But he was deeply
immersed in his work, scribbling notes in the margins of
the typewritten sheets with a silver-capped pen, and
paying no attention whatsoever to her.

Throughout the remainder of the flight he continued
to behave as if she were not there at all, and Melody
responded in kind. After the dinner was served and
cleared away, she closed her eyes for a while, though
sleep was far away, trying to relax.

'Excuse me, *fraulein*.' His voice brought her back to
the moment. He spoke, she noted, with a faint American accent, but beneath that, the slight inflexion of the
German-speaker betrayed European origins. 'Do you
require any duty-free goods—cigarettes, perhaps?'

Melody opened her eyes to see that the stewardess had returned with the duty-free trolley.

'No thank you, I don't smoke,' she replied automatically.

'Nor I,' he replied, but nonetheless he took his full allowance of tobacco. 'For a friend,' he explained. 'He always urges me to bring him my quota. Perhaps it is wrong of me to encourage him in his unhealthy habit.'

His tone was friendlier and slightly less distant than before, and Melody was encouraged to say politely,

'I expect your friend would buy them, anyhow, whether you brought them for him or not.'

The dispassionate blue-grey eyes regarded her steadily for a moment, and a grave half-smile deepened the creases at either side of his mouth, the lift of the fine, arched eyebrows emphasising the intellectual cast of his features.

'Oh, I am sure he would,' he agreed. 'But I wonder, does that fact, in itself, absolve one from guilt?'

He was speaking purely hypothetically, she assumed, examining the question in an academic manner, but Melody flushed, and turned once again to look out of the window. Did anything absolve one from guilt, she wondered, and felt a fleeting anger, directed at him, for having reminded her of things she would have preferred to forget.

The plane circled over the city below and began its descent. From this height, and in the darkness, Mozart's birthplace was only a pattern of spangled lights, but all the same excitement stirred in Melody, and she forgot her brief anger. She fastened her seat belt and braced herself for the landing, deliberately not looking to see if her companion had resumed his meditational pose.

After they had touched down, he stood politely aside

to allow her to precede him down the aisle. His eyes were once more distant, as if he were thinking of matters far more important than an unknown girl who had sat next to him on the plane, but he nonetheless bestowed a grave smile on her and said,

'I hope you enjoy our beautiful city.'

His words confirmed that he was a native of these parts, and he, of course, had mistaken her for a tourist.

'Thank you,' she said, suppressing an insane desire to cling on to him as to a lifeline. He was gone, swiftly swallowed up in the confusion of arrival, luggage, customs, and she did not expect to meet him again. At his own wish, they had exchanged only a few words, but she felt strangely alone when she lost sight of him, in this place where she knew no one else.

CHAPTER TWO

HER progression through the formalities was swift and trouble-free, speeded up, perhaps, by the fact that someone well-known and influential locally was waiting to meet her. A big man, broad but not fat, dark hair only just touched with grey, and a smiling, confident manner, he came towards her as she stood looking hesitantly around.

'Miss Cameron?'

'Yes . . . I'm Melody Cameron.'

His hand took hers in a grasp that almost made it disappear.

'I am Hugo Schulz. Welcome to Austria.'

Outside, a large and comfortable car was waiting. Melody's case was stowed in the boot, and she was helped quickly and efficiently into the front passenger seat. She leaned back, grateful for the ease with which this transfer had been accomplished, guessing that Hugo Schulz was a man used to getting things done his way.

The airport, as is usually the case, was well outside the city, and as the big car swung out onto a broad highway, she realised with a pang of disappointment that their route apparently did not take them through Salzburg itself. She would have to wait for a glimpse of the city for who knew how long? Sternly, she reminded herself that she was here to work, not to see the sights, but she did hope that at some point she would have the opportunity.

Leaving the lights and the bustle of the airport behind them, they turned off along a quieter road, with a great many twists and bends and, imperceptibly at first, they began to climb.

'It is a great pity that you arrived in darkness,' he said. 'You would enjoy this drive very much in daylight, it is highly scenic. But never mind—you will have the chance to see it all another time.'

As he drove, he drew her out to talk about her training and experience, which she did willingly enough, and it did not take her long to realise that in a subtle and unobtrusive way, she was being interviewed. So she answered his questions as fully and precisely as she could, and noted that he seemed satisfied with her replies.

Fortunately, he did not ask very much of a personal nature, only one brief question as to her family, and she replied quietly that she had none. Mrs Moore had assured her that the Schulz family would know nothing of the tragedy at the hospital—after all, it was scarcely relevant to the purpose for which they were employing her.

Hugo Schulz gave her a strange look, part curiosity and part admiration.

'You are young to be so alone in the world,' he remarked. 'Of course, from our point of view it is good that you have no ties and are free to devote yourself, but for you, it is sad. Is there not, perhaps, a young man to whom you are attached?'

'No young man,' she said emphatically. 'I am quite free, Herr Schulz, and I shall do all I can to help your daughter. Is she home from hospital now?'

'Yes, Kristina is already home,' he said, somewhat heavily, she thought. 'She is actually my stepdaughter, did you know? But as I have been married to her mother since she was small, she might almost be my own. We have a son, too, Max—he's ten.'

Melody acknowledged this fact, which she had not known. In fact, she knew very little about the Schulzes, as they did about her. They were taking each other very much on trust. She wondered briefly why they had chosen to employ a nurse all the way from England. There must have been many, locally, whose references they could check up much more easily.

Hugo almost answered her unspoken thought.

'I should warn you,' he said. 'Kristina can be a little . . . difficult.'

Melody smiled.

'I am used to that in patients, Herr Schulz. Anyone who has had to lie flat on her back for months, enduring pain and uncertainty, then undergoing traction, therapy, injections—to say nothing of the indignity of being helpless—can be expected to be difficult. How could it be otherwise?'

He paused.

'True, no doubt. But you don't, I think, understand quite what I am saying. Kristina has always been difficult. The accident has merely aggravated a natural tendency. I will be frank with you, since we are alone, and a little knowledge may help you to see the picture more clearly. My wife lost her first husband after a very brief marriage, leaving her only Kristina, whom she spoiled and indulged to a large degree, perhaps to compensate. By the time I came on the scene, it was too late to reverse the process, although I have tried to slow it down a little. Kristina is used to having her own way, and she is like the devil himself if she is crossed. Being helpless and in hospital has taught her neither patience nor humility. In fact, the entire staff was glad to see the back of her.'

He took a deep breath, straightened the car after taking one of the many twists in the road, and glanced at her out of the corner of his eye.

'There, now. I have been honest with you, but have I put you off, I wonder? Do you still want to go on with this?'

Melody gave a low laugh. Far from being discouraged, she found an element of challenge in what he had told her.

'I am not so easily deterred, Herr Schulz,' she assured him. 'In spite of what you say about your stepdaughter she is still a girl who has suffered a very bad injury. I have worked on a ward where we were used to spinal injuries, and I shall treat Kristina just as I would have treated my patients there—with the proviso that as she has been allowed home, she must be considered on the road to recovery.'

'I think I am going to like you, Miss Cameron,' he said, relieved. 'It will be reassuring to me, and to my wife, to have you around. I hope you will be happy with us.'

Melody smiled her slow, sweet smile. She hoped so too, although perhaps 'happy' was too strong a word. Could she ever hope for happiness again, after what weighed on her mind? Did she even have the right? If she could be busy, useful and content, then she thought she would be satisfied, and not ask for more.

By now, they had begun to climb higher. Melody felt the gradient increase as Hugo drove. The night was black, dull and moonless, and she sensed around her the presence of mountains she could hardly see, their looming bulk, the iciness of their high, alpine peaks. Now and then they passed swiftly through a village, a dazzle of lights, gone almost before she could register it. There was the glimmer of water beside them for short stretches of road, before that, too, vanished, and then, further on, yet another lake appeared.

'We are in the Salzkammergut,' he told her. 'In summer there are many tourists exploring the mountains and lakes, in winter, we have the ski-ing fraternity. Now we are past the time for good ski-ing, but scarcely into spring, so it is quiet. That was St Wolfgang we just passed through, made famous by the operetta *The White Horse Inn*. In August, of course, Salzburg has the Music Festival, and many of these villages are full to overflowing with visitors.'

Once again they were alongside a lake, water gleaming darkly, and reflecting the lights of a small but elegant town as they drove through.

'Bad Hallenstein, our nearest civilisation,' he said with a smile. 'It was once quite a flourishing spa, you know—the word *Bad* before a name usually denotes a spa—but not so many people come to take the waters, now. However, you will find it has adequate shopping and recreational activities.'

She glanced quickly at him, as if in protest, but he read her thoughts.

'Oh yes, we do not expect you to be tied to our daughter's side twenty-four hours a day, seven days a week. You must have your off-duty time, as any nurse would. Much of the time you will not be occupied with nursing duties, anyhow. The fact that you are here, if needed, will be sufficient. And the help Kristina needs is psychological as much as physical, according to the doctors.'

'That's usually the case with injuries such as she has sustained,' Melody observed.

The car was climbing quite steeply now, the town and

the lake left behind them, the darkness of the night and the mountains enclosing them. Hugo Schulz turned off through wrought-iron double gates into a curving drive-way and, round its bend, the lights of a house blazed into the night.

Mrs Moore had said that the Schulzes were 'quite prosperous', and Melody could only suppose that this was a typical British understatement—or, that, not hav-ing been here herself, she did not know how affluent Eva Schulz's second husband was.

The house seemed to grow from the very hillside on several different levels. In front of them, on the ground floor, were the garages, of which Melody counted three, and above that the first floor was a solid wall of glass. Although it was dark the curtains were not drawn, and as the interior was well lit, she could see that it appeared to be one immense room, running the entire length of the building. But the glass, which looked all of a piece, must in reality have been sliding doors, because there was a large, wrap-around terrace with a wrought-iron balus-trade.

He noted her quietly admiring gaze and said,

'You like it? I designed it myself, of course. It seemed crazy to have the living-room at ground level and miss the full beauty of the view, hence the garages under-neath. Some say it stands out like a sore thumb in these surroundings, but I don't see why we should have to have chalet-type houses with wooden shutters and win-dow-boxes, attractive though they are, simply because our forefathers did.'

He pressed a button on the dashboard, and the first of the garage doors opened silently and smoothly by re-mote control.

'A small refinement,' he laughed. 'It gets cold here, in

the winter, and one doesn't always want to get out and fumble with the doors.'

To Melody, who had known only the spartan drabness of the orphanage, and the uninspired bleakness of the nurses' home, all this was unashamed luxury.

'You have a beautiful home, Herr Schulz,' she breathed, trying not to sound wistful. To live in a place like this, for however short a time, would be an experience she would not forget.

'Save your verdict until you have seen the rest,' he advised, but his voice was confident. Clearly, he had an unshakable belief in himself and his designs, and did not expect either to be found wanting.

From the garages a passage led to a flight of steps leading to the first floor. He opened a door at the top and ushered Melody into a spacious hall.

'Come and meet my wife,' he said, and she followed him, with no time to take in much more than a general impression of warmth and space and elegance.

The room she had glimpsed briefly from outside was no less impressive now she was in it. In spite of a grand piano in one corner, and more seating than the nurses' common-room had held, it did not look crowded. Acres of gleaming parquet surrounded a glowing oriental carpet, the colours of which were echoed in the upholstery and the floor-to-ceiling velvet drapes drawn back from the windows. Lamps gleamed softly, recessed spotlights picked out the rich leather bindings of books and the abstract modern paintings on the walls, which Melody did not imagine were reproductions.

A woman sat in one of the plush armchairs, fondling the ears of a huge Great Dane sprawled at her feet. At their approach, both rose and came towards them. The dog slobbered mightily all over its master, and then sniffed inquisitively at Melody. She had never had the opportunity of owning pets and so had not had much to do with dogs, and she stood transfixed as this great creature rose on its hind legs and put its front paws on her shoulders.

The experience was a little unnerving, but she had an idea it would be unwise to betray the fact.

'Good boy,' she said, in the calm, reassuring tone she used for nervous patients, and the hound wagged his tail enthusiastically, and licked Melody's face with his great tongue.

'Down, Siegfried!' the woman said, and the dog obediently subsided to the ground.

'He likes you,' said Eva Schulz, and her husband smiled fondly at her and in a bantering tone said, 'That's just as well, for anyone Siegfried doesn't fancy might just as well pack his or her bags, right away.'

'Don't be silly, Hugo,' Eva said equably. He might be a rich and successful architect, a man of some eminence locally, but his wife was in no way intimidated by him, that much was obvious.

She stretched out a hand to Melody.

'How do you do?' she said politely. 'I hope you had a comfortable journey.'

She faltered a suitable reply, and the slim, cool fingers relinquished hers almost at once. Melody knew instinctively that this slender, silver-blonde, middle-aged woman with the patrician features and somewhat glacial eyes, was the real power, so far as she was concerned. Her gaze dissected the girl before her, so that Melody had the uneasy feeling that Eva Schulz could see into her very thoughts.

'Won't you sit down?' she said. 'You must be very tired. I expect you had dinner on the plane, but if you are hungry I'll have some supper prepared for you.'

Melody sank into one of the chairs. Her small frame seemed to go much further back than she had expected, and she wriggled forward again, trying to maintain a dignified position, hands folded quietly in her lap.

'Please don't trouble, I'm not at all hungry,' she assured her new employer.

'I'll get Lindi to take Miss Cameron's luggage upstairs, and then bring some coffee for us,' Hugo said.

With his large, confident presence gone from the room, Melody felt very much alone and at the mercy of this shrewd-eyed woman who was still calmly weighing her up. She told herself that Eva had a perfect right to do this. They had never met, and yet she was employing her to take care of her daughter. She resisted with much effort the temptation to fidget.

'Kristina is in bed, I'm afraid, so you will not meet her until tomorrow,' Eva said. 'She does tend to tire easily, and the doctors said she must have plenty of rest. Who would have thought that being in a wheelchair would be so exhausting?'

'It's the mental effort, Frau Schulz,' Melody ventured comfortingly. 'Rehabilitation is a long, slow process, and patients can easily become depressed by the sheer effort of it.'

Eva sighed.

'Not only the patients,' she said. 'Sometimes I wonder whether Kristina will ever walk and live normally again.'

'But surely,' Melody frowned, 'I understood that the spinal nerves were not severed, and her spine has healed well. There is every reason to hope, indeed to expect, that in time she will.'

'So you may think,' Eva said, a little sharply. 'No doubt you have seen many such cases, and to you this is just another. But Kristina is *my* daughter, and if *I* cannot persuade her the effort is worthwhile, I fail to see how you will be able to do so.'

Melody sat straight up, as if she had been slapped across the face, as the implication of the other woman's words gripped her. She had a cold, distinct sense of being unwelcome, something she had not expected, but the vibrations coming across to her from Eva Schulz were unmistakable. She swallowed hard, and quietly, patiently, she replied,

'I am a qualified nurse, Frau Schulz, and as you say, I have nursed patients with injuries similar to your daughter's. Every one of them was an individual to me, and I cared very much that they should have the best I could give. I don't dispute that a mother's love is something entirely different, but perhaps the fact that you love your daughter so deeply, with so much involvement . . .'

She hesitated, afraid that already she had said too much, but there was a glimmer of reluctant appreciation in the icy gaze that held hers.

'So. You are not such a little mouse as you might appear, Miss Cameron. Or has my husband already got to you? He, too, does not think I am the right person to care for my own child in her terrible need.'

She glanced at the gilt ormolu clock on the mantel-shelf.

'What *is* that wretched girl doing with the coffee? I am beginning to think she will have to go. But one cannot get good staff nowadays, they are all working in the hotels.'

She rose to her feet, walked across to the immense windows and pressed a switch. The glowing velvet drapes swept silently over the glass, shutting out the night.

'As you will have gathered,' Eva said coolly, 'it was not my idea to employ a nurse. In fact, I opposed it strongly. But my husband can be very stubborn at times, and in this he had the support of the doctors at the hospital.' She shrugged. 'I am not a fool, *fraulein*. I wish to do what is best for Kristina. So here you are . . . and we shall see.'

Was there something ominous in that 'we shall see'? Melody knew she would have Eva's coldly appraising eye upon her, whatever she did in this household. This job was going to have pitfalls and problems she had not suspected.

She was saved from having to reply by the return of Hugo, followed by a girl carrying a tray of coffee and cakes.

'Leave the tray, Lindi. You can go now,' Eva told her. Graciously, she poured coffee, added cream and sugar, dispensed cake. That brief display of hostility whilst her husband was out of the room might never have been.

As for Hugo, he sat on the arm of his wife's chair, smiling down at her, catching her gaze as it locked with his from time to time, as she talked easily of this and that, local customs and places of interest which might be expected to entertain a stranger. The couple might disagree on occasion, sometimes forcefully, but Melody could see that this was a strong and stable marriage, rock-sure and unshakable. Not like James and poor Liane, the unbidden thought came to her.

There could be no pleasing Hugo without pleasing Eva, for although he might put his foot down occasionally, as he had over Kristina's nurse, in the last analysis he would support his wife. So Melody was going to have to tread carefully and be very sure she did not offend that lady, whilst at the same time fulfilling properly her rôle as nurse.

Could she do it? She set down her delicate cup carefully on the onyx-topped coffee table, and as if sensing her uncertainty, Siegfried ambled across the room, and put his great, warm head on Melody's knee. Well, at least I have one friend here, the girl thought ruefully. And for tonight, it seemed she would have to be content with that.

CHAPTER THREE

THE spring sunshine was spilling through a gap between the curtains when Melody awoke to her first full day in Austria, and she lay looking appreciatively around her new quarters. She had never, even temporarily, occupied a room like this, in which all the furnishings spoke of unashamed luxury and comfort. The carpet was deep, shaggy pile in a pale gold colour, which was reflected in the bold modern print of the curtains and bedcovers. She had her own washbasin, vanity unit and mirror, and her bed had a fitted headboard complete with bedside table, reading lamp and radio. There was a deep, comfortable basket chair by the window, dressing table, bookshelf, and a vast wardrobe, in which Melody's few clothes looked forlorn and lost. It was a far cry from the orphanage and the nurses' home, and she reminded herself firmly that all this was only hers on loan, so to speak. The time would come when she would have to give it up and go back to what she had known before, so it would be as well not to become too attached to this affluent lifestyle.

Unable to contain her curiosity any longer, she got out of bed, padded barefoot across the carpet, which scrunched deliciously under her toes, and flung open the curtains.

'Oh, my giddy aunt!' she gasped irreverently. Last night's arrival in the dark had not prepared her for this. She was looking directly down the hillside towards the arm of the lake they had skirted briefly by car. Only now it shimmered and sparkled in the sunlight. A brisk breeze capped the wavelets with white, tossing them into a merry dance. The little town nestled by the shore of the lake, and mighty green hillsides sloped down to meet it on every side. The mountain peaks were still snow-capped, and long white fingers of winter stretched down into the valley, but the blue sky promised warmer days to come, very soon. Neat fields covered the lower slopes, with picture-book chalets dotted here and there. Melody could not have bitten back her exclamation of delight even if she had wanted to.

After a long while spent gazing enraptured at this scene, she tore herself away and looked at the clock on the bedside table. It was almost seven o'clock, and she decided it might be as well to dress and be ready for whatever the day might bring.

It seemed strange not to be putting on the familiar blue and white uniform. She had mentioned the question of dress to Eva Schulz the night before, mainly to ascertain if Kristina's mother had any preference as to how she should be attired, and Hugo had answered quickly, before his wife had a chance to speak.

'Uniforms are essential in hospitals, not only to make staff easily identifiable, but to prevent infection, I suppose,' he said. 'But Kristina is not in a sick-room situation now, and we all know who you are. So just wear ordinary, sensible clothes, Miss Cameron. We want you to live as one of the family.'

Melody was not at all sure that was what Eva wanted, but she did not contradict her husband on this occasion. Only a brief tightening of the firm lips betrayed that she had any thoughts whatsoever on the subject.

So now Melody had a wash and dressed quickly in a plain woollen skirt and a cream blouse, choosing sensible, low-heeled shoes. She brushed her mid-brown hair into its habitual neat, shining page-boy, put on her watch, and the gold chain James and Liane had given her at Christmas, the only good jewellery she owned. Make-up? No, she decided. Just a flick of warm pink lipstick would be sufficient.

She was examining herself critically in the mirror when a clear, imperious voice called out from the room next to hers.

'Nurse! Nurse—come here, I need you now.'

Melody straightened. Her room was next door to Kristina's, she had been told, as it would have to be if she was to be of any use, but she had moved around very quietly, and hoped she had not awakened the girl. Still, she was eager to meet her patient, and did not allow herself to be put off by the note of arrogant impatience in the voice which summoned her.

She tapped lightly on the inter-connecting door, and opened it, saying cheerfully, 'Good morning. I hope I didn't disturb you.'

Then she stopped, abruptly, as if she had come up against an invisible barrier.

Kristina's room was at least twice the size of her own, and correspondingly more luxurious. Everything was in shades of blue, from powder to navy, through periwinkle and cornflower and a deep shade that was almost indigo. The girl had her own television set, walls full of cupboards and shelving, and an open door showed an *en suite* bathroom—blue, of course. A moody and dramatic room.

But it was not the room which held Melody fixed to the spot. It was the girl herself, lying back against a jumble of pale blue pillows. She had a small, heart-shaped face with a pointed little chin and *retroussé* nose, surrounded by a leonine mane of tumbled blonde curls almost to her shoulders, slanted golden eyes that snapped fire, and a mouth which betrayed all too readily the demanding, self-centred nature of its owner.

To look at her was like seeing Liane over again. Younger certainly, and richer, but her face was formed to the same specifications. Here, too, written on that face, Melody recognised the same greedy, volatile temperament, reaching out restlessly to take, at all costs.

How could fate have been so cruel, she wondered, still reeling with astonishment and dismay. She had travelled clear across Europe, to a new life, only to be reminded and haunted by what she had thought to leave behind. For a few moments she simply stood there, recovering from the blow which the sight of this girl had dealt her.

'Well?' Kristina Schulz demanded impatiently. 'Are you the new nurse or aren't you? I sincerely hope you aren't going to stand there all day with your mouth open.'

Melody snapped back to life.

'I'm sorry,' she said. 'You have rather a striking resemblance to someone I used to know, that's all. Yes, I'm the nurse. My name is Melody Cameron, and I'm pleased to meet you, Fraulein Schulz.'

The girl's expressive features contorted into a grimace.

'Ugh! You aren't going to be all stiff and starchy, and remind me of that dreadful hospital, are you? My name is Kristina. And I shall call you Melody. Now, having got that out of the way, I should like, not unnaturally, to go to the bathroom.'

The long years of training and discipline stood Melody in good stead. She put the moment of shock resolutely behind her, and helped Kristina out of bed, gently but capably.

Her patient was slimly built and far from heavy, and Melody knew exactly how to lift and support her, but she had the unmistakable impression that Kristina was being about as uncooperative as she could be.

'Ouch! Melody, you're hurting me! You nurses have about as much feeling as blocks of granite!' she complained.

'That's because you are resisting me, Kristina,' Melody said, patiently but firmly. 'If you go with me, instead of against me, you will find it much less painful.'

'It's all very well for you,' grumbled the girl. 'People think because I'm sitting down most of the time nothing hurts, but that's not so. I'm sore in places you wouldn't like to mention, in spite of that wretched rubber thing they gave me to sit on, and my legs—sometimes the pain is excruciating.'

'The pressure sores I can do something to relieve,' Melody told her. 'As for your legs, I know they hurt, and I know the pain-killing tablets only help up to a point. But that's the healing process. Would you prefer to feel nothing, and know you would be confined to a wheelchair for the rest of your life?'

The golden eyes slanted up at her with an unreadable expression.

'But I *am* going to be confined to a wheelchair. Don't think you can fool me with that professionally cheerful attitude, any more than they could at the hospital. I'm never going to be the way I was before.'

'Whoever told you that?' Melody asked lightly, as she eased her patient into the bath.

'No one told me, I just know it.' Kristina, up to her

neck in scented bubbles, stared up at Melody as if daring her to defy that edict.

Melody took a deep breath. She knew that the first step in this girl's recovery must be made by herself—she must believe she could walk again, and put her will, her effort, her faith to work. And Melody must not for a minute go along with this defeatist attitude.

'All I can tell you is, I've nursed patients like you who are now up and about their business again,' she said briskly. 'I'm not saying it was quick or easy for them, but they made it, and so can you.'

The effort of the bath appeared to have exhausted Kristina for the moment, and she did not appear to have any inclination to get dressed.

'I usually have my breakfast in bed,' she informed Melody. 'Would you go down to the kitchen and tell Frau Schmidt, or Lindi that I'm ready. Second door on the right, and *frühstück* is the word, in case you're wondering. Neither of them speaks English.'

'My German is a bit rudimentary, but I'll manage,' Melody said wryly.

She went down the wide, softly carpeted stairway to the hall, and into the large, well-appointed kitchen where the girl who had brought the coffee the night before and an immensely fat, middle-aged woman, were busy preparing breakfast. Lindi, whose fate it seemed to be always behind schedule, was being berated by the other woman, and her young face was red and flustered as she hurried to prepare Kristina's tray.

Seeing that the poor girl was busy, and already in trouble, Melody took the tray from her, and indicated that she would take it up to Kristina. She was rewarded by a grateful smile.

'How nice,' Kristina murmured, as she entered. 'I'd

much rather you bring my breakfast up than Lindi. She generally slops coffee on the tray, or drops something, and I can't abide clumsiness.'

Very probably she was in terror of the sharpness of Kristina's tongue, Melody thought, and she realised that by her sympathetic act, she had acquired a job for the duration of her stay here. Not that she minded. She had dished out no end of meals on the ward in much busier circumstances, and the more contact she had with Kristina, the sooner she would get to know her. She settled the tray on her patient's bed, adjusted the pillows behind her, and asked if there were anything else she wanted.

'No thanks. You'd better go and have your breakfast. The dining-room is next to the kitchen. Perhaps you could draw the curtains just a little on your way out—too much light in my eyes. Oh, and pick up that pile of magazines from the floor, would you?'

Waitress, lady's maid, and what else, Nurse Cameron? Melody smiled to herself as she made her way back down the stairs.

The long, elegant dining-room overlooked a formal garden where roses would bloom in the summer, and beyond a trelliswork screen Melody caught a glimpse of a swimming pool. Seated at the shining mahogany dining table, Hugo Schulz, in dark business suit, was drinking coffee and flicking through a newspaper. On his left, a boy with his father's dark hair and his mother's slimmer build was spreading rolls liberally with jam. Of Eva, there was no sign.

Hugo smiled at her.

'Good morning, Miss Cameron. Everything is all right, I trust?'

'Everything is fine, Herr Schulz,' she assured him. 'Kristina is having breakfast in her room.'

His eyebrows rose.

'Already? Curiosity must have woken her early,' he remarked. 'This is my son, Max. Max, this is Miss Melody Cameron, who has come to look after your sister.'

The boy grimaced cheerfully.

'Good luck, Miss Cameron,' he said. 'Kristi will give you . . . how do you say in English, a run for your money.'

'Max!' his father reproved mildly, and Melody looked down at the table to hide a smile. She wondered if the boy would have said that if his mother were present.

Hugo folded up his newspaper and got to his feet.

'Come on, son. I'll give you a lift down the road, or you'll be late for school. No, you don't really want another roll.'

Max grinned at Melody and followed his father out, the bread roll still in his hand.

Alone, Melody poured herself a cup of coffee and helped herself to one of the freshly-baked rolls. It was very pleasant to sit here, in this charming room, enjoying a leisurely breakfast whilst looking out into the garden, and for a moment she was lulled by a sense of ease, forgetting her demanding patient upstairs with her uncanny likeness to the dead Liane.

The soft click of the door opening roused her from her daydream. It was Eva, immaculate in a slim grey pencil skirt and soft pink silk shirt, a scarf of muted greys and pinks knotted at her throat. She favoured Melody with her cool little smile and slipped into her chair.

'Good morning. More coffee? Yes, I think so.' She refilled Melody's cup before attending to her own. 'You have already met Kristina, I gather. I make a point of seeing my daughter first thing in the morning, and she tells me she is still bruised from her session in the bathroom.'

Melody was about to laugh, assuming this to be a joke, albeit in rather poor taste, but meeting Eva's eyes, she saw there was no humour in them.

'I . . . I was extremely careful,' she stammered, taken aback by the unexpected note of accusation. 'We're taught how to lift patients so as not to cause them more discomfort than necessary, and . . .'

Eva waved an airy hand.

'Please. I know the layout of the rooms is unfamiliar to you, and I told Kristina we must make allowances for that. We will say no more about it, only do take extra care, won't you? She has already suffered enough.'

'Of course.' Wrong-footed so skilfully, there was little Melody could say in her own defence without bringing up Kristina's deliberate lack of co-operation, and that, she felt, would be mean-spirited of her. She drank her coffee in silence.

'I have to go out this morning,' Eva said at length. 'Now you are here, there is no reason not to resume activities I have neglected since Kristina came out of hospital, and there is a courtesy visit I must make. Are you sure you can cope?'

'I am quite sure, Frau Schulz,' Melody said, politely but firmly. 'That, after all, is why I am here.'

Eva gave her a long, measuring look which stated quite clearly that she did not believe for one moment that Melody could look after Kristina as well as she could herself.

'Quite so,' she said. 'You will excuse me.'

She left the room, and Melody noted that she had eaten no breakfast at all, and that half her coffee was still in its cup. She had come to the dining-room for one purpose only, to shoot her small dart of criticism at Melody, and having done that, she was satisfied.

Melody sighed, and met the tentative, sympathetic smile of Lindi, who came in to clear the table. Between you and me, that smile said, transcending the barriers of language, this is not an easy household in which to make a living.

She went back upstairs to help Kristina dress. Was she imagining it, or was there a challenge in the slightly mocking expression in the golden eyes. Yes, I told my mother you were rough with me in the bathroom—go on, confront me with it, it said. But Melody chose not to mention the incident. She had to win Kristina's trust, and did not think launching into a spate of accusations would help her to do so.

It was no easy job getting Kristina into her clothes. The girl blocked all her efforts with a kind of passive resistance, an inertia which Melody was fairly sure was deliberate. Kristina could help herself a lot more if she chose to. Was her refusal to do so a way of making life awkward for Melody, to see how much this new nurse could take? There might be an element of that in it, Melody thought, but she believed the roots went deeper. Kristina had convinced herself, and was endeavouring to convince everyone else, that she would not be able to lead a normal life again.

Why? Melody wondered. Because she was by no means convinced, quite the contrary, and if there had to be a battle for this girl's recovery, then she was prepared to fight. Whilst she sat over her coffee that morning, Melody had come to terms with Kristina's resemblance to Liane. Not that it was going to go away. Every time she looked at that face, it would remind her, and if ever there was a penance, Melody felt that this was hers. But she was strangely sympathetic towards the aggressive, vital personality confined to a wheelchair, denied the full outlet of her youth and beauty. Ultimately, she had been unable to deflect Liane from her urge to self-destruction, but she would do all she could to prevent Kristina from resigning herself to life as a cripple. This one, she told herself firmly, I *will* help.

Not that it was going to be easy. It was a major battle, to begin with, to get Kristina, complaining mightily, down the stairs and into her wheelchair.

'My father didn't design this house with paraplegics in mind,' she groaned. 'Too many steps, owing to its being built on the hillside, of course. They wanted to move me to a ground floor room, but I absolutely refused. Give up my beautiful room, and my view—no way!'

And Kristina's refusal would be accepted, no matter how difficult it made life for herself and everyone else, Melody thought ruefully. Still, she could understand her attachment to her own room, and the splendid vista of mountains and lake.

'You are *not* a paraplegic,' she said equably. 'Sooner or later, you will walk down those stairs on your own. I went on a course dealing with rehabilitation methods not so long ago, and naturally we always worked closely with the physiotherapist. I'll show you some leg exercises which will strengthen the muscles you've been unable to use for so long.'

Kristina grunted contemptuously.

'A waste of time,' she declared. 'Still, I suppose you have to earn your money, and it can't do me any harm.'

'That's right,' Melody said cheerfully. 'Now, tell me, since I'm new and don't know your routine, what do you plan to do for the rest of the morning?'

'Keep the patient happy, Nurse,' jibed Kristina. 'Oh,

I don't know. I shall probably read or sketch, so I shan't need you hovering round me all the time. Why don't you take Siegfried out for a walk? He's looking a bit anxious, and I'd guess no one's had time for him this morning.'

At the sound of his name, the huge dog came and stretched out in front of Melody, with his head on her foot, a plaintive howl emanating from his throat.

'Do you think he'd go with me?' she asked doubtfully.

'Oh, surely. Look, you've already made a conquest. And don't worry about getting lost. He knows the way, and its always the same.'

Melody enjoyed the brisk ramble up the hillside, with the dog trotting obediently at her side. For such a large animal he was extremely biddable, and she risked letting him off the leash for a run around. Fortunately, he came back the instant she called him, and as Kristina had said, knew exactly the route he wished to take. She returned to the house with a glow lending colour to her usually pale cheeks, and a sparkle in her eyes.

Her happiness in the moment evaporated, however, as she encountered Eva, with a disapproving expression on her face.

'It is going to be difficult to rely on you, Miss Cameron, if every time I venture out for an hour or two, you disappear, leaving my daughter alone,' she said plaintively.

'I only took Siegfried for a walk,' Melody faltered. 'We were gone for only a few minutes, and Frau Schmidt and Lindi are both in.'

'Nevertheless,' Eva insisted, 'I would prefer you to be here if I am not. You will be given ample free time, I assure you.'

The inference, clearly, was that Melody could not wait to leave her charge and go swanning off around the countryside. But that was unfair! She had only walked Siegfried, they had never been out of sight of the house, and it had been at Kristina's instigation, anyhow.

Kristina! She had propelled herself out into the hall, and over her mother's shoulder her eyes met Melody's, with a hint of cruel laughter. You fell for it again, they said. And so she had. For whilst it was not true, as Eva had hinted, that she was anxious to be off enjoying herself, she *had* left Kristina alone. It was unlikely that the girl could have come to any harm, unless she had wilfully brought it on herself, but with Kristina, who knew? She would have to be doubly careful.

'It won't occur again,' she said quietly, accepting the reproof with as good a grace as she could muster.

'Very well. Do join us for lunch, Miss Cameron, as I hope you will for all meals,' Eva said graciously.

Lunch was a simple but excellent meal of cold meats, salad, fruit and coffee. Neither mother nor daughter ate a great deal, Melody noted. In Eva's case, it was surely her own affair, but Kristina needed the energy provided by good food to build her up, and Melody tried, discreetly, to encourage her to take more.

'Don't fuss, Melody, I'm not hungry,' she said testily.

'Miss Cameron is right, *liebchen*,' Eva said, for once backing Melody. 'You should eat more.'

'I don't see how you can expect me to have much appetite, *Mutti*, when I don't do anything to make me hungry,' she pointed out, reasonably enough.

'I know, darling. It is difficult for you, but you must try.' Eva's eyes melted with love and compassion. Which was all very right and natural, Melody thought, but it wouldn't solve the problem. What Kristina needed was exercise, stimulus, involvement. She would give it some

thought, she decided, but for the moment a little fresh
air could not harm.

'The sun is shining. It might be an idea for me to take
Kristina out for a while,' she suggested.

'But she might catch a chill,' protested Eva.

'Not if she's well wrapped up, and we don't stay out
too long.'

They both looked at Kristina, who lifted her shoulders
eloquently.

'Oh, why not? I suppose it would be a change to look
at a different view, and be out in the open air,' she said
indifferently.

'Very well then, *liebchen*, if you wish, but you must
have your rest this afternoon, particularly as we have a
guest for dinner.'

'One of Papa's boring colleagues, I daresay,' Kristina
groaned. 'I think I shall plead tiredness and eat in my
room.'

'I think you will not. It's Dieter von Rheinhof,' her
mother said triumphantly.

The girl's bored expression underwent a miraculous
transformation. She sat up straight, her eyes sparkled
with life and verve, and her lips curved into a smile.

'I was beginning to think I should have to accuse him
of gross neglect!' she said. 'It's ages since he came to see
me.'

'It's not above a week, Kristina. And he has been
away. He only got back yesterday from the conference
he was attending. I saw him this morning and invited him
to dinner.'

'Did he ask after me?' Kristina demanded at once.

'*Natürlich*, he asked how you were. It is an indication
of his affection that he accepted my invitation so soon
after he has arrived home. He would not leave

Heiligenkreuz again for just anyone!' Eva's eyes twinkled, meeting those of her daughter with ready complicity.

Kristina tossed back her mane of curls and laughed triumphantly. Her sullen listlessness had vanished completely. Whoever this Dieter von Rheinhof was, he must be very important to her, Melody decided.

The brief spell out in the fresh air brought colour to Kristina's face, and after an enforced rest in the afternoon, she was in a state of febrile excitement deciding what to wear. Melody could see her problem. The vast, walk-in wardrobe was spilling over with dresses, coats, suits and jackets, there were drawers full of sweaters, racks of shoes, there were riding habits, ski-ing gear, swim-suits, all the accoutrements of someone who has led a very active life, physically and socially.

'You're wondering how I ever found time to wear them all,' Kristina said shrewdly. 'Well I did, I can assure you. Half of them could be given away to charity now, for all the use they are.'

'Fashion doesn't change all that quickly,' Melody smiled.

'Not in riding gear, it doesn't, but I don't expect to need that again. So let's concentrate on choosing something to gladden the eyes of Professor Doktor von Rheinhof.'

Melody's eyes widened with interest.

'He is your doctor, this guest who is coming to dinner tonight?'

Kristina's laugh pealed out.

'Goodness, no, not *my* doctor. Dieter doesn't specialise in broken bones, but in broken minds.' She pointed to her forehead with an expressive gesture. 'He's medical director of a psychiatric hospital, at Heiligenkreuz, a few miles up the valley. I'm surprised you haven't heard of him. He's a very eminent psychotherapist, travels all over the world presenting papers at conferences, writes learned tomes and lectures at universities.'

'He sounds most impressive,' Melody said. 'And he's also a friend of the family, I gather?'

'You could say that. I've known him since I was a child. He taught me to ride and to ski. I can't remember a time when he wasn't part of my life.'

She pointed to a dress of glowing emerald green silky material. 'That one, I think, don't you?'

'It's a lovely dress,' Melody agreed. She helped Kristina to struggle into it, and then had to suffer recriminations because her hairstyle had been ruined. Kristina pinned it up again with swift, impatient fingers. She looked very lovely, with the blonde curls piled on top of her head, cascading in unruly profusion over her forehead, and her eyes shining, a glint of green somewhere in their depths. Beside her, Melody felt very ordinary.

But then, she thought, an eminent psychotherapist is not coming poste-haste from a conference to visit *me*. She immediately rebuked herself for the thought. She had her health and strength, and a chance to remake her life. To ask for more would be criminally greedy, she decided guiltily, but could not help wondering what it felt like to be aglow from within just because a man was coming to dinner.

Downstairs in the spacious lounge the lamps were already lit, and the last of the light was draining from the sky outside, leaving the outlines of the mountains stark and cold against the evening pallor. Max grinned up at Melody from where he lay sprawled on the carpet reading a book, and Siegfried thumped his tail in welcome as she wheeled Kristina in.

Hugo was just pouring a glass of sherry for Eva and himself.

'For you, too, Miss Cameron?' he inquired politely. 'Dry or medium?'

'Oh . . . er, medium, please,' she stammered, a little unsure of herself in this sophisticated household.

'And me, too,' Kristina insisted. 'Oh, come on, Papa, don't be a spoilsport! I'm not on medication now, unless you count those wretched pain-killers, which are worse than useless.'

Hugo looked at Melody.

'What would you say, Miss Cameron?'

She cleared her throat nervously.

'I would say that in moderation, it can't do any harm.'

'You see!' Kristina was triumphant as she accepted her glass. 'And her name is Melody, by the way, and that is what we are going to call her.'

Hugo smiled, apparently relieved to find his stepdaughter in a livelier mood.

'Of course we shall call her Melody, if she does not object to the informality,' he said.

'Oh, please, I'd much prefer it,' Melody said quickly. Being addressed as 'Nurse Cameron' or just 'You! Nurse!' on the wards, was one thing, but here the formality of hearing herself addressed as 'Miss' had unnerved her, and thinking they preferred it, she had not known how to change matters. She was grateful to Kristina for breaking the ice.

'You are looking very lovely tonight, my dear,' Eva smiled fondly at her daughter. 'I always thought that colour suited you.'

Her gaze flickered briefly over Melody, who had

changed into a dress of fine cream wool. It might not look very special to the Schulz women, with their extensive wardrobes—Eva, tonight, was coolly elegant in black crêpe de chine—but it was the best she had. She hoped they would not be doing too much entertaining or else everyone, herself included, would be heartily sick of the sight of That Dress, she decided ruefully.

'Dieter is late,' Kristina said irritably, fidgeting in her chair.

'I expect he has a lot to catch up with on his first day back,' Eva said soothingly.

'No matter. He knows I look forward to seeing him, and I don't have a great deal to look forward to,' the girl said petulantly.

'This must be him, now,' Hugo said, as a car's headlights swept the driveway outside.

Melody heard the bell ring and Lindi go to answer the door, and curiously, she waited for her first glimpse of this man who was so important to Kristina. Then, as he entered the room, she stifled a gasp of astonished recognition, for Dieter von Rheinhof was none other than the man who had sat next to her on the plane!

CHAPTER FOUR

She had a moment or two to recover from her surprise, as the newcomer greeted the family, shaking Hugo's hand and giving Eva the polite continental kiss on the cheek, not forgetting a comradely smile for Max, and a pat on the rump for Siegfried, who shivered with joy in welcome.

'Kristina, *kind*!' His long stride brought him swiftly across the room to the girl in her wheelchair, and he bent to offer her the same salutation he had given her mother. But Kristina clasped both her hands possessively at the back of his head, drawing him down and returning the kiss with fervour.

'Dieter! Oh, it is so good to have you back!' she murmured.

'All this after only a week! I can see I shall have to go away more often,' he said, lightly, jokingly, defusing with kindness and discretion the intensity of emotion in her welcome. But he submitted to the embrace without demur, and no one in the family seemed in the least surprised by it.

Straightening up, he came face to face with Melody, and she found herself meeting once more that penetrating, blue-grey gaze she remembered all too well.

Kristina still had a firm, clinging grasp on one of his hands.

'Dieter, this is Melody Cameron, whose ill fortune it is to have to cope with me,' she laughed a little breathlessly, and across the months, the echo rang in Melody's

52

brain . . . *my new friend and guardian angel* . . . She bit
her lip so hard that she tasted blood, forced the memory
to the back of her mind, and turned her attention to
Dieter von Rheinhof, a welcoming smile of recognition
ready on her lips.

But he was looking at her in precisely the manner one
looks at a stranger to whom one has just been introduced, polite, interested, but detached, as if her face
meant nothing to him. Melody's smile died, to be re-
placed by a faint frown of puzzlement; she found it hard
to believe he truly did not recognise her, or had forgotten their previous encounter after so short a space of
time.

It was in her mind to say, 'But we met on the plane—
don't you remember?' But she never framed the words.
He had his back to the rest of the company in the room,
and over Kristina's golden head, so that only Melody
saw it, his features tautened into an expression that
forbade her to mention their meeting—the merest,
almost imperceptible shake of the head, and a compres-
sion of the firm lips, but the meaning was eminently clear
to her. He did not want it known that they had already
met.

Melody was under no obligation to comply with this
silent request—no, it was not a request, more of a
command—for secrecy. His manner towards her on the
plane had been alternately kind and forbidding, and now
he wanted her to pretend that the encounter had never
taken place. Why should she do any such thing, Melody
wondered defiantly. She was already under sufficient
stress in this household, and had no desire to subject
herself to more. But she could not rid herself of the
conviction that whatever this man might do, there would
be some good, sound reason for his behaviour, although

she herself might not know what that reason was. He inspired a certain trust and confidence, and it was because of this that she held her peace.

'I am pleased to make your acquaintance, Miss Cameron,' he said, briefly taking her hand. The long, tapering fingers were cool and dry, she noted, it was an extremely well-kept hand that held hers, firmly masculine and in no way effete.

She scarcely knew what she answered, but was fortunately spared having to say too much by Hugo, who remarked,

'It's very odd, Dieter, but when we passed each other briefly at the airport the other night, I was there to collect Melody. You must have come in on the same flight.'

Eva cast her husband an oblique, warning glance that suggested he was lacking in diplomacy.

'That's possible, but one doesn't notice everyone who travels on the same plane with one,' she said coolly.

'Quite,' said Dieter von Rheinhof, with calm aplomb. 'For most of the flight I was, anyhow, immersed in my conference notes,' he added, quite truthfully.

Melody, by now, was totally confused. Both Eva and the eminent specialist were at pains to establish that although he and the English nurse may have travelled on the same flight, they had had no contact with one another, whilst Hugo was clearly not wholly in tune with this conspiracy. Only one fact emerged with any clarity—somehow, at the hub of all this, was Kristina. She was the one for whom the pretence was being maintained. But why? Her adoration for Dieter was obvious and unconcealed, but surely she could not be jealous of such an unimportant incident, to the extent that her mother and Dieter would go to such lengths to deny that it had taken place!

Glancing at Eva, Melody was shocked to see on her face an expression of pure hatred, directed at herself, as if the whole thing were her fault, which, in a way, the girl supposed that it was. Swiftly, the smooth mask covered it, Eva smiled and said,

'Hugo, I'm sure Dieter would like a drink, and in the meantime I shall go and ask Frau Schmidt how dinner is coming along.'

The mahogany table in the dining-room was elegantly set with a formidable array of gleaming cutlery and fragile looking crystal wine glasses at each place. An attractive centrepiece of winter greenery enlivened by a few dark red roses, no doubt extremely expensive at this time of year, decorated the table, along with a branched silver candelabra. Melody, who was nervous in case she dropped or spilled something, or said the wrong thing, nonetheless could not resist exclaiming aloud at the effectiveness of this.

For once, Eva's smile was genuine.

'You like it? I arranged it myself.'

'Very much. It's basically so simple, and yet so eye-catching.'

'I always do the flower arrangements. If you are interested in such things you may help me,' Eva said graciously. 'Lindi is useless for this, and Kristina, for all she loves painting and sketching, has no talent for doing things with her hands in a practical sense.'

'I should be pleased to,' Melody said promptly. It was the first sign Eva had given of accepting her into the household, and she was glad of it. Not that she was naive enough to believe that henceforth all would be plain sailing, but at least it was a step in the right direction.

For most of the time during dinner she spoke only when directly addressed, even though the entire party spoke English exclusively, out of courtesy to her. Admittedly, it did not seem to be any hardship to them. Kristina was truly bi-lingual, having been taught both languages from birth, and largely educated at English schools, and everyone else was quite at home in the language. Even Max had a good grasp of it, and was rarely stuck for a word. But much of the talk was about people Melody did not know, and local matters of which she was ignorant, so she kept quiet.

She was acutely aware of Dieter von Rheinhof, whose behaviour towards her had been so puzzling, and oddly enough, it was he who finally drew her into the conversation, asking her questions about her training, and what kind of nursing she preferred. Melody answered politely and fully, because she loved to talk about nursing, and because, however upset she might have been by his manner, it was not in her nature to bear malice. More and more she grew convinced that Kristina was at the bottom of all this. She made it clear she did not like his attention focused on Melody for too long, and steered the discussion back to subjects on which the English girl could not converse whenever she could.

But there was no denying that she blossomed in his company, and it was possible to see the gay and vital individual she had been before her accident. Whilst she was seated at the table, talking and gesturing animatedly, one could forget for a moment that she was confined to a wheelchair. Eva had known what she was doing when she invited this man, his effect on her daughter could be compared to that of a life-enhancing drug.

In this distinctively European household there was a long, Germanic tradition of respect for education and academic prowess, and Dieter von Rheinhof was clearly accorded this kind of respect by all, even by a man such as Hugo Schulz, who was successful and wealthy. Money was not the touchstone, nor, ultimately, was birth, although Melody knew that the prefix *von* before a name indicated a background of gentility. But this man was more than an honoured guest, more than an old friend in the Schulz household. He was welcomed and accorded the affection, almost, of another son.

Kristina seemed as if she could scarcely have enough of his presence, of the sight, sound and touch of him. Her adoration reached out to envelop him with avidly grasping tentacles. He did not deny her, but his response was measured, controlled, and Melody thought that this would be a hard man to possess, even for those he loved. He had an inner core of reserve into which he seemed able to withdraw at will, and he lived primarily for his work, that much was obvious from the way he spoke of it.

Melody shook her head as Hugo would have refilled her glass. She was not accustomed to wine as an automatic partner to a meal, to her, it was a special occasion habit. Here, it was just taken for granted as the thing to do, and she guessed it would take her some time to get used to it.

She listened attentively as the talk went on, ranging through politics, literature, art, and finally, to music. And here she caught a glimpse of Dieter's second great passion. He glanced up and surprised her watching him as he told them of a splendid concert he had been to in London, his enthusiasm almost infectious, and he regarded her steadily, unperturbed by her covert scrutiny.

'My love of music is no great secret in this household,' he said. 'As for yourself, with a name like Melody, you should also have some affinity with it—a musical parent, perhaps?'

She found herself blushing absurdly.

'Oh no, nothing like that. It's a silly name, isn't it?' she heard herself babbling apologetically. 'It was given to me by the warden of the orphanage where I was raised, who must have had a romantic streak somewhere. But yes, I do enjoy music.'

'What is unusual is not necessarily foolish,' he said. 'The lady had imagination—Melody.'

Melody found that all her senses were cast into total disarray. On the plane he had been aloof and distant, when they met before dinner he had pretended he had never seen her before in his life. And now, his repetition of her name, spoken with that fascinating accent, caused her heart to somersault ridiculously, she did not know why. It was unfair. Furthermore, she had never thought of herself, her name, or her background as even remotely romantic. If anyone had asked her to describe herself, she would have said she was average, nondescript, unremarkable. It was madness to let this attractive, distinguished man cause such disquiet within her, merely by speaking her name.

'You were brought up in an orphanage, Melody?' Kristina broke in, curiously. 'Have you no idea who your parents were?'

'None whatsoever. I was left outside the maternity hospital in a carrycot, and they gave me the surname of the Scottish ward sister who found me there,' she said lightly, wishing now that she had not inadvertently brought up the subject.

'How very picturesque,' Kristina said, toying with the stem of her wine glass. 'Don't you think so, Dieter?'

He smiled.

'You have a very dramatic turn of phrase, but it's hardly the word I would have used myself. However, one could say that it is a testimony to Melody's strength of character that she has made her way in the world, alone.' He turned to Melody, the smile becoming slightly quizzical. 'Perhaps that is why you chose to become a nurse—the hospital fulfilling the rôle of family?'

There was nothing flowery about the compliment he had paid her—it was intended merely as a statement of fact. It was, after all, this man's profession to look into the minds and motives of others, and exercise judgment on what he saw. All the same, her cheeks were tinged with pink as she replied.

'I think you are right about the hospital, at any rate.' she admitted. 'I believe I did find security there.'

'Then why leave it?' Kristina demanded sharply, with uncanny shrewdness.

Melody's smile covered her sudden confusion—or at least, she hoped it did. Kristina's intelligence was too sharp for her own good, and Dieter von Rheinhof was not a man to be fooled easily. But what could she tell them? She could not bring herself to say, 'I left because two people died, there were those who held me in part responsible—and who is to say they were wrong?'

'There comes a time for everyone to leave the safety of the family, and strike out on his or her own,' she said. 'To stand on one's own feet, and know whom one really is.'

It was not the whole truth, but as she said it, she knew that neither was it a lie. That time would most likely have come for her at some point, even if it had been thrust upon her by the tragedy of her friends' death. Whether Kristina, or Dieter, for that matter, accepted it as her real reason, she could not be sure, but somehow, she did not think either of them did. Kristina's doubt was almost palpable, a sharp, vicarious need to probe into Melody's dark places. His, on the other hand, was more a suspension of belief, a professional reservation of judgment. But it was to him that she wanted to protest her innocence, strangely concerned lest he should draw his own conclusions about her reasons for being here, and think badly of her.

They all adjourned to the lounge for coffee, and then Max was reminded by his mother that he had homework to finish before bedtime. He grimaced a little, but gave in with good grace and said his goodnights all round before leaving them.

'Why don't you play the piano for us, Dieter?' Kristina urged. 'It is so long since I heard you play.'

'It is precisely for that reason that I should not do so,' he excused himself. 'It is so long since I had the time to play, and my fingers are stiff and out of practice.'

'You always say that, but you always play beautifully,' she rejoined. 'Won't you do so, now—to please me?'

'If you put it like that, how can I refuse?' he smiled, moving over to the piano with the long-limbed grace which characterised all his movements. The long, flexible fingers slid easily over the keys, and the room was filled with a Chopin nocturne. Kristina sat by his side, waiting to turn over the pages, and it was impossible not to see what a heart-catching picture they made, the man with his fine, intelligent face, and the girl with her cascade of blonde curls high on her head, her golden eyes watching him intently. No wonder Eva was smiling at the pair of them with complacent maternal fondness.

A lump caught in Melody's throat. She did not know whether it was on account of this perfect little cameo, or because the music seemed to express a wistful longing, which ran like a thread of sadness through all life. She longed for something at that moment, but she could not have said what it was. To belong somewhere . . . to be necessary to someone's life . . . yes, but that was not the sum of it. Just beyond her ability to express, it hovered, waiting for her understanding to reach out and grasp it. And she could not quite do so.

'We shall meet again, no doubt,' Dieter von Rheinhof said to her, before he left. For a moment, no one was watching them, and he added quietly, 'When we do, I shall not forget that I owe you an explanation.'

She said hastily, 'It doesn't matter,' and in a tone which stated plainly that he expected no contradiction, he said,

'It does to me.'

She flinched at the note of arrogance in his voice, and watched the lines of his face soften into tender affection as he took his leave of Kristina. For some inexplicable reason, this brought on a recurrence of the sadness she had felt whilst listening to him play.

'Come soon,' she heard the girl whisper to him. 'You know I can't bear it when you are away too long.'

'I am a busy man, *liebchen*, as you know,' he replied, 'but I shall be here whenever I can, have no fear.'

Melody helped Kristina to bed, seeing that she was comfortable and hanging up the green silk dress in the copious wardrobe.

'Did you like him?' Kristina asked. It was not necessary to ask her to whom she was referring.

'He . . . he seems very nice,' Melody said guardedly.

Even to her own ears, the word sounded inadequate and totally unsuitable as an adjective to describe Dieter von Rheinhof, and Kristina pounced on it with contempt.

'Is that the best praise you can find? What more does a man need to arouse your enthusiasm? He's handsome, clever, talented, he comes from an old, aristocratic family, and he's rising fast in his profession.'

'And those qualities are more important than any personal assets, such as kindness and understanding, which he also might possess?' she could not resist saying.

The blonde eyebrows arched over the golden eyes in an expression which reminded Melody unmistakably of Eva.

'*Touché*, Melody! You're quite smart, underneath that innocent exterior, aren't you? The point is, they are qualities which are important to my *mother*. To me, Dieter is . . . just Dieter. There's no one like him. You know, of course, that I'm going to marry him.'

There was an empty, sinking sensation in the region of Melody's heart. Of course, she might have known—the girl's open adoration, her intense possessiveness, and his tender solicitude.

'You're engaged?' she asked, trying to make the query sound light.

'Not formally. But then, we don't go in for things like that here. It is not strictly necessary. Everyone has always known that we would marry,' Kristina told her confidently. 'My parents are in agreement, his mother has also expressed her approval, and what's more to the point, he is the only man I have ever wanted. And a man like Dieter von Rheinhof is far too honourable to ditch a girl simply because fate has confined her to a wheelchair, wouldn't you say?'

Melody closed the wardrobe door and picked up Kristina's hair-brush from where the girl had dropped it.

'All the more reason for us to do our best to get you

out of the said wheelchair so you can walk down the aisle with him,' she said calmly.

Kristina's face contorted in sudden anger.

'No!' she cried vehemently. 'That can't be done, and you know it can't! And even if it could, it would take years! I'm not going to wait that long to marry Dieter, nor will he expect me to. He'll take me as I am!'

'But—' Melody began, on the verge of explaining that the process she had in mind was measured in months, not years, if the patient were willing and co-operative.

Kristina turned her head on the pillow, closing her eyes.

'Go away, Melody,' she said wearily, her anger evaporating as swiftly as it had flared up. 'I've had enough for today. And you really don't know anything about Dieter and me,' she added dismissively.

Melody closed the door softly and returned to her own room, reflecting that this, at least, was true. She knew nothing of the relationship between these two before Kristina's accident, or of the long-standing, unofficial agreement to marry at some future date—after all, Kristina was still very young—approved by both families and interrupted by an unfortunate mishap. Behind Dieter's smiling reserve no doubt he loved the girl as passionately as she adored him, but he was holding back, treading gently on account of her disability. Why else would he endure her possessiveness, to the point of hiding from his fiancée the insignificant truth that he and Melody had sat next to one another on the plane?

What puzzled Melody was that if she were in Kristina's place, with a man like that patiently awaiting her recovery, she would be doing everything in her power to get out of that chair and on to her feet, to regain her independence and resume her rightful place in the world. But Kristina was doing just the opposite, and it simply did not make sense.

CHAPTER FIVE

THE sun was warm and bright, causing Melody to blink a little as she strolled along the lakeside promenade. Spring had arrived all at once, sudden and rapturous, melting the lingering snow on the foothills and bringing people out of their hibernation to smile at one another with shared appreciation, as if to say, 'Yes, it's here, isn't it wonderful? We thought it would never come, but it has.

She had been more than two weeks with the Schulz family now, and had adapted herself swiftly to the routine of their days. In the morning, there was breakfast to take up, after a brief, but increasingly confident conversation with Frau Schmidt, who came in each day to cook. Lindi, who lived in, cleaned, served coffee, and did what Melody thought of as general 'dogsbodying'. Then she helped Kristina to bath, dress, do her exercises; took her out for a walk in her chair if it were fine, or a drive in Kristina's own car if it were too cold to walk. She supposed it was nursing, although it was a far cry from the bustle and discipline of the wards. Still, it was caring for a patient's well-being. The family doctor, an old and trusted friend who had known Kristina many years, called occasionally and discussed any points he thought she needed to know, although the girl was still officially under the care of the hospital, and would have to make return visits from time to time to see the specialist there. He prescribed some different pain-killing tablets when Melody told him Kristina complained the ones she had were scarcely easing the pain.

'Surely she should have some callipers, to help her get around on her feet a little, by now?' Melody said questioningly, and he frowned a little.

'She already has them. She is not using?'

There was nothing for it but to ask Eva, who admitted that yes, they had the callipers, but Kristina refused to use them.

'Take those ugly things away!' she had screamed. 'I am not going to hobble around on those!'

When Melody tried, her response was more or less the same.

'I'm not going to use those things, so you might as well put them back in the cupboard,' she said flatly. 'My legs still hurt far too much, anyway.'

'They will, to begin with, but you should try to bear it, and persevere, if only for a few minutes at a time, at first,' Melody explained. 'Unless you make the effort, you are never going to walk again.'

'That's what I have been trying to tell you since you arrived here,' Kristina said, a triumphant gleam in her eyes.

'And I have been trying to tell you that the remedy is in your own hands. We can all help you, but only *you* can provide the effort.'

'I can't. I'm not ready.'

'You mean you aren't prepared to try,' Melody said. 'Can't you remember when you were in hospital, flat on your back, and then what a struggle it was just to sit in a chair for a while? But you did it. Now you're saying that all those doctors and nurses who worked so hard to make it possible for you to come as far as you have wasted their time, and you aren't going to justify their efforts because you simply can't be bothered!'

Kristina stared furiously at her for a moment, and then, without a word, she spun the chair around and propelled herself out of the room.

Eva, who had been standing in the doorway, listening to this little exchange, came in, aghast and horrified.

'Miss Cameron . . . Melody!' she snapped. 'How could you talk to her like that! You know how much she has had to bear! I always imagined nurses to be kind, caring people, but just then you were so hard and cruel!'

Melody sighed.

'Sometimes, one has to be cruel to be kind, Frau Schulz,' she said. 'In spite of all her family's love and attention, in spite of being jollied along and pampered and encouraged, Kristina is still right where she was when she left hospital. It could be that we have to shock her out of that helplessness, make her angry, galvanise her into action. I've seen tactics like that work when all else has failed,' she added reassuringly.

'You came to us very highly recommended, and I don't doubt you have much experience of hospital methods and procedures,' Eva said, 'but I can't stand by and watch my poor child castigated like that!'

Melody said, 'Frau Schulz, I don't need to ask if you want to see Kristina walking again. The question would be pointless. The doctors think she can do it, and for what it's worth, so do I. Isn't it worth a few tears, if it gets her on her feet?'

'I see your point,' Eva said. 'But what if you are wrong? Maybe Kristina is afraid to try, because it might turn out to be all for nothing, and then she will have to add disappointment to her trials.'

'Unless she makes the attempt, she will never know,' Melody pointed out, gently. 'And nor will you.'

Eva had turned away and said no more, but Kristina

had remained adamant in her refusal. It was not, Melody thought, that she was afraid to try, rather, she was determined not to.

She sighed, as the breeze from the lake ruffled her hair, and brought her back to the present. This was supposed to be her day off, but it was hard to keep her mind off her problems. Even harder than it had been on the wards, for now she lived with her patient twenty-four hours a day, and for better or worse, was becoming increasingly involved with her.

That morning, she had caught the small, local bus, which came down the main road into town from the mountain villages.

'Take my car,' Kristina had said idly. 'No one uses it these days.'

But she had been reluctant to do that—it was tanta- mount to saying Kristina herself would never drive it again, and she had protested that she quite liked travel- ling on these little country buses, which was true. The bus had disgorged its passengers in the town's main square, and she had wandered happily about the streets, admiring the quaint shops and interesting corners, the sudden glimpses of blue lake visible at every other turning. Now, standing on the promenade, gazing out across the lake, she tried to imagine what it would be like in summer, with its small bathing beach crowded with frolicking holidaymakers, and sailing craft of all kinds on the water.

'Hello! *Wie geht es Ihnen, heute, Fraulein?*'

She had no need to turn to recognise Dieter's voice, but she did so all the same, and stood, silhouetted against the blue lake and the green slopes beyond, quite unaware of the picture she made with the breeze blowing a strand of hair across her cheek.

'*Es geht mir gut*, Herr Professor,' she responded politely. She had seen him twice since the night he came to dinner when he called briefly at the Schulz house, and on the second occasion she had complained that her German was not progressing as swiftly as it might, since only Lindi and Frau Schmidt ever spoke it with her.

'You responded quickly enough to that,' he told her, in English.

'Oh, I'm learning—slowly,' she said. 'What one learns in school is never as relevant as one thinks it will be in a real situation. And both yourself and the Schulzes speak English so excellently, it makes me feel ashamed.'

'There is no need,' he pointed out, reasonably. 'The circumstances are quite different. You have been here a matter of days, only. Eva was married to an Englishman, and lived in England for some time after his death. That, in fact, was where she met Hugo, who was in partnership with a firm of British architects for a while. Kristina, of course, is half English. As for myself, I lived and studied in the United States some years ago.'

'Which explains . . .' Melody began, and then stopped.

'Explains what? Do go on.'

'I was only going to say, it explains why you speak with a slight American accent.'

He considered this for a moment. 'Do I? Yes, I suppose I must do. We never really listen to ourselves talking. Occasionally I have taped a lecture, and been horrified that the voice I heard was my own.'

Listening to the controlled and beautifully modulated voice, Melody found that difficult to believe, but of course, she did not say so.

'As a matter of fact, Melody,' he said, 'I am glad I happened to see you today. I have not had the opportunity to speak to you alone, and I wanted to explain to you why I gave the appearance of not knowing you that first evening.'

'Really, there is no need,' she said swiftly.

'But there is. You must have thought me unpardonably rude, and with some justification, and I want to make things clear to you. Come and have some coffee—we can't talk seriously out here in the street.'

'I don't think . . .' she began, but he ignored her protest, took her arm, and led her along the promenade, then back along a narrow street leading to the square. Melody gave in gracefully, realising he was used to having his wishes complied with. When a man reached the heights which Dieter von Rheinhof had attained, particularly in the medical profession, a certain arrogance, which was almost regality, hung around him like a rich cloak.

However, he gave no outward appearance of having overridden her wishes, and chatted amicably about the welcome warmth of the day, and the fact that he had just come from an appointment with his lawyer where he had been dealing with a small query concerning some property belonging to his mother. By this time, they had come to a small *Stüben*, cosy with dark wooden settles arranged in alcoves for privacy, and he ushered her towards a window seat, looking out on the square.

The coffee was good and strong, served with thick cream, and he had ordered delicious chocolate cake to accompany it. She did not think Dieter's lean, energetic frame would alter, however much Sachertorte he ate, and only prayed that hers, too, would withstand the onslaught of life in Austria, where such delights were an inevitable part of almost every day. However, since it was put in front of her, and she could hardly refuse, she ate it with enjoyment.

'How pleasant to see a young woman who appreciates food,' he said. 'So many just pick at it.'

'It's hardly surprising, with cake such as this,' she laughed. 'It's a wonder all Austrians aren't as fat as pigs. But you aren't. Perhaps there's an inbuilt immunity,' she suggested.

'A nice thought. The man who invents the antidote for obesity will make a fortune,' he said.

All this casual chat was merely postponing the real purpose for which he had brought her here, she knew, and he must have realised this too, for his expression grew suddenly serious. Anxious not to waste his valuable time with any more small talk, she said,

'I understand—about why you had to pretend we had not met—really, I do.'

The finely arched eyebrows rose slightly.

'You do?' he said, and those two words, phrased as a question, put Melody in the awkward position of having to explain his motives to him, and she stumbled on, uncomfortably.

'Because of Kristina. Because you thought that she might be jealous—quite needlessly, of course.'

'Of course,' he agreed equably, and quite readily, and she thought ruefully that he need not have rubbed it in that a gorgeous creature like Kristina Schulz had no need to be jealous of anyone as ordinary as Melody. 'Kristina's moods are . . . shall we say, volatile, at the best of times,' he explained. 'These are not, for her, the best of times, and incidents which have no significance in themselves can assume an importance which is quite disproportionate. I believe the maintenance of her mental equilibrium is an essential part of her recovery. To put it simply, I did not wish to rock the boat. I can only thank you for having the presence of mind to play along with me.'

Melody sat silent for a while. It was not especially pleasant to hear him confirm that their initial meeting had been, so far as he was concerned, an 'insignificant incident', for all she knew this to be so. She did not for a moment expect to have made a deep impression on him, although she could not honestly deny the impact he had made upon her.

'I think you credit me with more agility of mind than I in fact possess,' she said, as coolly as she could. 'The truth is, I was too surprised to do anything else.'

She wasn't going to admit to this man, who could be charming one instant and full of a distant hauteur the next, that she had picked up the message his eyes had so commandingly flashed her, and obeyed it instinctively.

'So?' said Dieter von Rheinhof. The faint curve of the finely chiselled lips suggested that he did not entirely believe her, but he did not press the point. 'Then shall we leave it at that, and discuss it no further?'

And that, she realised, was exactly what they would do. The subject had been raised by him, aired to his satisfaction, and then dismissed—again, by him. Melody experienced a brief flare of rebellion against this benign autocracy he so effortlessly wielded. It was a novel and somewhat alarming sensation, for although they were not within the confines of a hospital, she was still a very junior nurse, and he a doctor of consultant status.

'Very well,' she heard herself saying, with some horror. 'Perhaps I had better go now, since if Kristina knew we were having coffee together, it might assume an importance out of all proportion.'

The blue-grey eyes studied her with an apparent laziness which was quite deceptive.

'I am supposed to find that remark humorous?' he asked, and the quiet voice had a cutting edge like honed steel. 'Forgive me, I had thought we were being serious, not merely facetious.'

Melody took a deep breath. She knew she had over-stepped the mark, and there was nothing for her to do but retreat gracefully.

'I'm sorry,' she said quietly. She felt small, and dimi-nished, and for one awful moment thought she was going to cry, but when she looked across the table, he was smiling at her—calm and without rancour, almost sym-pathetic.

'Drink your coffee,' he said, 'and tell me what you are going to do with the rest of your day.'

She swallowed, and got a grip on herself.

'I hadn't made any definite plans. I expect I shall just wander around, looking at things. That's what I like to do, and as it's the first time I've been here, I expect I shall find plenty.'

'Certainly you will. You can take a steamer across the lake, if you wish to get a better view of the mountains. Or if you like architecture, there is a beautiful little baroque church just off the Markstrasse, and a square with a perfect Biedermeier-style drinking fountain.'

Melody, who had spent many of her off-duty days back in England exploring churches and old buildings, cried enthusiastically,

'Oh, I should enjoy that! Where exactly are these places?'

'My day is booked solidly with consultations from the minute I return to work, so I am afraid I cannot spare the time to show you around,' he told her, and she sensed again that withdrawal at which he seemed so adept. Aghast that he might have thought she was fishing for an invitation, she said quickly,

'Oh no, I did not mean . . . I only wanted you to tell me! You must not feel obliged . . .'

'Don't be apologetic, Melody,' he said, with a faint smile. 'I did not feel obliged, I would have been happy to show you the sights, but I genuinely am busy.'

She was in such a turmoil of embarrassment that she scarcely understood the precise directions he gave her to help her find the places of interest. Gently, he said,

'I think you have temporarily lost interest in architecture. If you prefer more up to date amusements, there is a very good indoor swimming pool.'

Melody forgot her own preoccupations, and her eyes brightened as she seized on this remark.

'Is there really? I haven't come prepared to swim today, but it might be an idea to bring Kristina. Swimming is marvellous exercise for the leg muscles, and would help her, I'm sure. Besides, she should get out a little.'

His smile lit up the austere, intellectual features as if a lamp had been switched on inside a room.

'That would be an excellent idea, if you could convince her, and persuade Eva to let you bring her,' he said. 'I also find it encouraging that you are thinking about Kristina, even on your day off.'

'I don't switch off for twenty-four hours, just because I'm off duty,' she said, rather more briskly than she had intended. 'I don't think anyone does, and I'm quite sure you don't, Herr Professor.'

'I don't,' he admitted, 'although I do *try* to, since without at least some recreation, I should soon be of very little use to my patients. And I hope you are not going to carry on addressing me as "Herr Professor", for if you do, I shall have to call you "Miss Cameron" and I rather like the sound of "Melody".'

Melody flushed. His eyes were intent on her now, gravely smiling, and yet revealing a quality of intimacy she found disturbing. The lean fingers were close to hers on the small table, and she was aware of a strange impulse to reach out and touch them.

She drew back her hands and clasped them sedately on her lap. Ridiculous—what could she be thinking of? She hardly knew the man, his interest in her was perfunctory, and in any event, he was strictly off limits for her. He was going to marry Kristina, and soon if the girl and her mother had their way. Her life revolved around him, and he was as essential to her as breathing.

In view of all that, he should not be looking at her with that tender, almost caressing gaze . . . Or she should not be imagining that he was, she rebuked herself firmly. Could one imagine such a thing? Melody had had her share of admirers, none of whom had meant a great deal to her, but a man had never looked at her in quite that way before, as if he were building up an image of her in his mind.

Without transferring his gaze, Dieter raised his hand and summoned the waitress to bring more coffee. Melody knew she should make some excuse and leave, but the hot, steaming fragrance of the fresh coffee gave her a reason to stay, and she found herself grasping it with something like relief. Not yet, she thought. In five minutes, perhaps, or maybe ten.

'I thought about what you told us the night I came to dinner,' he said. 'About not knowing who your parents were. I found it a very touching story.'

'Please. I'm used to it now,' Melody said. 'When I was

very young, I used to fantasise that my real mother would come and claim me, but as I grew up I accepted that she either didn't want me, or for some reason could not keep me.'

'The latter, most likely,' he said. 'Very few mothers willingly abandon a child.'

'That's what I told myself. I don't feel any resentment. I hope she's happy, whoever she is, and doesn't still worry about me and what she did.'

'You are a very compassionate person, Melody,' he said, and she was conscious of a rush of guilt, so overwhelming she thought he must see it in her eyes. Compassionate? Maybe, but where had it led her? And was it compassion that caused her to be sitting here, spinning out the minutes with a man who was committed to the girl whose welfare was supposed to be her prime interest?

'I'm no angel, believe me,' she said tersely.

'I'm sure you are not, but then, which of us is?' he countered. 'None of us is without fault, and most of us have at least one thing of which we are ashamed and would prefer the rest of the world did not know. Don't carry a heavier burden than you need to, Melody.'

Was it then so obvious, she wondered, averting her eyes, that she carried one at all? Or was it only so to him, skilled in the devious convolutions of the human mind?

The coffee was finished. He paid the bill, and they walked out together into the sunlit street.

'I hope you enjoy your day,' he said. 'I must get back to work now. As I told you, I have a full schedule—and also an overflowing desk. Have you ever done any psychiatric nursing, Melody?'

'No, never. But then, it's a very specialist field.'

'I'm glad to hear you say that, because there has been

a tendency, of late, to think that a mind which is malfunctioning is on a par with a sprained ankle, or a duodenal ulcer,' he said. 'Of course, mind and body are closely interdependent, I should be the last to deny that. One influences the other. But for the patient suffering from paranoid schizophrenia, shall we say, his cure is by no means straightforward or assured. In spite of all the recent advances, I still feel like a blind man, tapping my way along with a stick. Sometimes I know what it is that I touch. Sometimes I guess, and am right or wrong. Often, I am simply going up a blind alley.'

Her eyes widened at this frank confession of uncertainty.

'Goodness, if *you* feel that way, how must everyone else in your field view the situation?' she wondered.

'They would view it a little more clearly if they admitted more often that they don't have answers, only hypotheses,' he replied, with a touch of grimness.

Then he smiled at her again, as they stood islanded on the busy pavement, with shoppers milling around them.

'You must excuse me, it's fatal to set me off on my favourite topic,' he said. 'It is endlessly absorbing to me, of course, but not necessarily so for others.'

'But really, I find it most interesting,' she said. 'I should like to know more.'

'You would?' He looked down at her from his height, and there was just a suspicion of mockery in his voice, as if he did not quite believe that her interest was purely medical. 'Are you asking me to unravel the mysteries of psychotherapy a little further for you? In that case, my next move should doubtless be to ask you to have lunch with me when you next have a free day.'

Melody suppressed a gasp. How dare he insinuate that she had any such end in mind? She burned inwardly at

the thought, but what made it worse, and took the wind
out of her indignation, was the fact that she found the
prospect so inviting, and would dearly have loved to be
in a position to avail herself of it.

She drew herself up to the full extent of her diminutive
five foot three, and met the veiled irony in his eyes
directly.

'I very much doubt that you would extend such an
invitation. At least, I hope you would not do so,' she said
primly.

'Would you have me believe that if I did, you would
refuse?' he said. His half-humorous tone of voice indicated that he found this possibility unlikely, and Melody
found her cheeks blanching with an anger that was rare
to her. She may have been young, and inexperienced,
and alone in a foreign land, but that did not give him the
right to assume that she was eager to grasp at compan-
ionship with any man who offered it—particularly with
one who was already promised to someone else.

'Naturally, I should refuse,' she replied steadily.

'I am devastated,' he said, with the same insufferable,
smiling calm. 'But for curiosity's sake only, would you
mind telling me why you would not take me up on my
hypothetical offer?'

She had the distinct awareness that deep down he
knew she wanted him to ask her, and knew she wanted to
accept, and she found this knowledge mortifying.

'I'm sure you'll understand, if you give it a little
thought!' she burst out. 'I may be only a nobody who
does not even know who her parents are, but I'm not the
sort of girl you seem to have mistaken me for!'

She turned and ran blindly, pushing her way through
the throng of shoppers, darting up side streets and
through quiet squares which seemed remote from the

activity of the main thoroughfare. She ran for several minutes until she was quite lost, and then finally stopped and collapsed, breathless, on a low stone wall. This was so silly. He must have ceased following her long ago, if, indeed, he had followed her at all. Most likely, he had simply shrugged his elegant shoulders and thought what a naive and ridiculous girl she was, and gone on his way without troubling himself further.

The bright day was now quite ruined for Melody. She had no desire for any of the things she had promised herself—a stroll round the town, lunch in a restaurant, a trip on the lake. They had all lost their savour, and for a moment, she almost hated Dieter von Rheinhof for taking the enjoyment out of her innocent pleasures, for making her aware that there were other pleasures, far more complex and rewarding, beyond those she knew and contented herself with.

Had he been serious, and ready to follow up his suggestion if she had appeared willing, or had he been merely teasing her? Melody was still far from sure how to take him.

A man like Dieter von Rheinhof is far too honourable to ditch a girl simply because fate has confined her to a wheelchair, Kristina had said. Possibly, but Dieter himself had said, not half an hour ago, 'None of us is without fault, and most of us have at least one thing of which we are ashamed'. He loved Kristina, and would stand by his commitment, but perhaps occasionally, he felt he needed the company of a woman who was not in a wheelchair, who was fit and healthy and able to walk at his side.

But it would be unwise to cast Melody in this rôle, even briefly. Only this morning, he had stated that where Kristina's emotions were concerned, he had no wish to rock the boat, and a good deal of turbulence would be caused were Melody to go out on a social occasion with Dieter, whilst Kristina sat at home in her wheelchair. Or had he expected the whole thing to be conducted in secrecy? If so, that demanded a level of sophistication Melody knew she did not possess.

The more she turned it over in her mind, the more convinced she became that he had never had any real intention of asking her out. Perhaps he really believed that she, in a roundabout manner, had been trying to put him in a position where he would feel obliged to do so. Melody tingled with embarrassment at the very idea.

The last thing she needed was to be drawn into a relationship with a man who belonged to someone else. Even friendship, as she had learned to her cost, could be misconstrued. She could not avoid seeing Dieter, since he was a frequent visitor to the house, but she could make it plain by her manner that she had no special interest in him.

And she hadn't, Melody told herself firmly, as she found her way back to the main square and caught the bus home.

CHAPTER SIX

'YOU'RE home early,' Kristina remarked, her eyes scanning Melody inquisitively for a reason.

'My feet ache,' Melody lied. 'I think I did too much walking.'

'You should have taken the car,' Kristina pointed out.

'Perhaps I will, next time. Why don't you come with me? We could swim at the indoor pool.'

'Swim?' Despite herself, there was a world of longing in that one word. 'What, me—swim?'

'Why not? The water will make you buoyant, and you'll find you are much more mobile. Leg exercises done in the water will be good for you, too.'

'Oh, but what a bore, getting the wheelchair in and out of that place, and getting me actually into the pool!' Kristina shook her head. 'You don't want all that performance.'

'Kristina, that's what I'm here for,' Melody reminded her. 'Besides, I should like to go swimming, and I don't fancy going alone. My German isn't up to coping with attendants and so forth.'

'Your German is perfectly adequate, and improving every day, and you don't fool me for a minute with that approach!' Kristina said sharply.

Nevertheless, it was she herself who brought the subject up at dinner.

'Oh, I don't know, *liebchen*,' Eva said warily. 'Are you sure it's even possible? Those places are not con-

81

structed for people in wheelchairs, and Melody would
have a dreadful time coping.'

'I told her that, but she says she can manage.' The
more Eva hesitated, the more determined Kristina became, which was the most hopeful sign Melody had yet
seen. 'After all, *Mutti*, why is Melody here, otherwise?'

'That's so,' Hugo said emphatically. 'I think you
should go, Kristi. Swimming will be good for her, won't
it, Melody?'

'It's recognised therapy, Herr Schulz,' she told him.
'One of the best forms there is. And it will be fun, too.'

She saw from his face that she had struck a chord
somewhere, and he held her back as the others were
going into the lounge for coffee.

'What you said just now made sense,' he said. 'Being
young is at least partly about having fun, and all that
seems to have come to an abrupt end for Kristina. I don't
think that necessarily has to be so, although obviously
there are limits to what she can do.'

'I wondered about that,' Melody frowned. 'She's so
pretty, and obviously a live-wire. Doesn't she have any
friends?'

'Friends!' Hugo snorted. 'That girl knows half the
province! They used to be up here in droves, honking
their car horns, and playing their ghastly pop music, they
almost sent us crazy! And she would be zipping off in her
car, half the time never telling us where she was going or
when she would be back. Ski-ing and skating in winter,
dancing, swimming, riding—' he checked himself, re-
membering how his stepdaughter had come to be the
way she was.

'What I am trying to say is that Kristina is not, by
nature, a recluse. But since the accident, she doesn't
want to see any of her friends. Won't let them come to

the house and visit, doesn't phone them up. She's cut herself off, and sees only us, and Dieter, of course. It is as if, since she can't have her life exactly as it was before, she won't accept a substitute.'

'I see.' Melody was thoughtful. 'Perhaps the swimming will be a first step in the right direction.'

'I hope so. Sometimes I feel she's not making any progress at all. But it has made an enormous difference, having you here,' he said. 'At least Eva is a little more free. She was getting so wound up with the girl, I thought she might crack up herself. You're getting on all right with Kristina, so it would appear?'

'We have our moments,' Melody told him, with a little smile. 'But yes, I think we understand one another.'

'Talking about me, were you?' Kristina asked irrepressibly, as they came in to join the others.

'Just arranging about the swimming,' Melody grinned. 'We'll go tomorrow.'

And they did, although not without a few moans from Kristina when Melody helped her into her swimming costume.

'Just look at me—this thing is hanging on me where it used to fit like a glove!' she complained. 'I shall certainly never make Miss World at this rate!'

'There's nothing wrong with your figure,' Melody said. 'You'll have lost a little weight, I expect, but you'll put it back. I told you, you could do with eating more.'

But it was worth the hassle of getting there, of coping with the chair and all its difficulties, once they got in the pool, and Kristina had the delight of regaining in the water something of the use of her limbs. After half an hour of this, Melody decided regretfully that they had better come out, and there was disappointment on the other girl's face.

'Oh, come on, Melody! Already? I've just got going.'

'I think it's enough, for the first time. We can come regularly, say once a week, and gradually work up to a longer session.'

Dried, dressed, and in her wheelchair once more, Kristina did look a little drained of energy, although she would not admit it. After so long in a prone or sitting position, the effort involved in any kind of mobility was considerably tiring.

'Hungry?' Melody asked hopefully. 'I know *I* am. Point me in the direction of a good restaurant.'

Kristina frowned.

'Can't we go home? You can't take me in a restaurant in this thing.'

'I don't see why not. People do. So long as there aren't stairs to negotiate we can manage. After all, now we are here we might as well finish off the morning properly.'

They passed several restaurants on the main street that Melody considered suitable, but Kristina would have none of them, and the one she finally directed them to was tucked away in a back street. Then she insisted on a very secluded corner table, and manoeuvred herself so she presented her back to the rest of the room.

She's ashamed, Melody thought, with a prick of sympathy. Her pride won't allow her to be seen like this, especially by anyone she knows. That was why she had wanted to go home, and had chosen this out of the way place. But Kristina was only nineteen. She couldn't shut herself off from the human race for the rest of her life. Even those who knew they were to be permanently disabled picked up the threads of their lives and tried to carry on as normally as possible. And having seen her in the water that morning, Melody was even more convinced that this was not so in Kristina's case.

However, all her precautions to avoid being spotted did no good. They were just finishing their lunch when Melody saw a dark-haired, very good-looking young man enter the restaurant. He glanced in their direction, hesitated, looked again, and then made his way towards them, his expression full of recognition and delight.

'Kristina! I knew it had to be you! Even from the back, there's no mistaking that glorious mane of yours!' he declared exuberantly.

'Hello, Klaus,' she replied woodenly. 'How are you?'

'I'm fine. Still working my fingers to the bone in my father's business. And you?'

'I am as you see,' she said, with a shrug. 'Melody, this is Klaus Becker, an old friend. Klaus, this is Melody Cameron, my nurse. She's from England, so please speak more slowly.'

'I am pleased to meet you, Miss Cameron.' Courteously, he spoke in English. He had a frank, open face, and a charming smile, and Melody found herself liking him. 'So you are looking after Kristina?'

'As much as she will permit me,' Melody smiled.

'She's a positive tyrant,' Kristina glowered. 'Come along, Melody—have you asked for the bill?'

'But we ordered coffee and it hasn't come, yet,' Melody said.

'No matter.' She pulled a handful of notes from her purse. 'Pay the bill. I'm ready to go.'

'Do stay and have coffee,' the young man begged. 'I haven't seen you in months. You won't speak to me when I phone, and you don't go anywhere we used to go.'

'I'm hardly in a position for ski-ing parties in the mountains, or dancing the night away,' she said, with cold sarcasm. '*Herr Ober!*' She clicked her fingers for the waiter, and pressed the money into his hand. 'We have to go now, Klaus. *Auf Wiedersehen.*'

She turned abruptly, and began propelling herself down the aisle between the tables. Melody felt sorry for the young man, who looked crestfallen, but she could see she would have to help Kristina, who, in her hurry to get out, was in danger of knocking a table over.

'*Es tut mir leid,*' she said hastily. 'I'm sorry, but we must go. It was nice meeting you.'

Kristina's face was taut, white and angry as Melody pushed her back to where they had left the car, and Melody herself was still quivering with embarrassment over their abrupt flight from the restaurant. She helped Kristina into the car, folded up the chair and stacked it in the boot, then got into the driving seat and buckled herself in, still without a word having passed between them.

Only when they were clear of the traffic in the town, and on the road back home, did Kristina say tersely,

'In future, Melody, we will go to the pool, swim, and come straight home. No lunches in restaurants, no hanging about. Understand?'

'If you wish,' Melody said, as calmly as she could. 'But I truly don't see why you have to hide yourself away. You're an attractive girl, and your friends obviously miss you. It was a shame the way you snubbed Klaus Becker just then.'

'I really don't want that boy mooning over me,' Kristina said emphatically.

'Boy? He's an extremely personable young *man*, I would have said. And clearly fond of you.'

'Listen, Melody, I know you mean well,' Kristina said, 'But it's no use my trying to get back the life I had before this happened to me. That's over now, and I'd rather make a complete break.'

'It's your business, Kristina, if you choose to turn your back on people who were your friends and would be glad to continue that friendship. But I think you're making a big mistake.'

'As you said, it's my business,' Kristina said curtly. 'In any event, I shall soon be married to Dieter, and then I shan't need anyone else.'

Melody licked her dry lips.

'Even people who are married need friends,' she ventured. 'Two people just can't live entirely through each other. It isn't healthy.'

Even as she spoke, she found herself thinking, she will want from him the same measure of commitment that Liane so mistakenly demanded from James.

'What do you know about love, Melody?' Kristina asked contemptuously. 'The kind of love in which someone is all the world to you?'

'I don't know anything, not from personal experience,' Melody confessed. 'But I had a friend who thought as you do, and it . . . it ended badly.'

Kristina tossed back her blonde mane.

'Your friend wasn't married to Dieter von Rheinhof,' she said. 'But I shall be, and then nothing else will ever be able to hurt me again.'

There was no way Melody could answer. Maybe Kristina was right, and once they were married, she would have a tender and considerate husband, who would understand her and shield her from all possible harm. She would, of course, have to share him with that other great love, his work—insofar as Kristina was capable of sharing anything she regarded as hers.

The spring sunshine was warm across Melody's shoulders as she drove. That being so, she wondered why she was shivering.

The morning's expedition had tired Kristina more than she had expected, and she was quite willing to take a rest that afternoon. Melody settled her in bed, and glancing in a few minutes later, saw that she was fast asleep.

She went downstairs a little aimlessly, feeling restless and not sure how to occupy this hour or so of leisure. Eva was out, Frau Schmidt had gone shopping, and apart from Lindi, who was busy cleaning somewhere, she had the house to herself. Except Siegfried, of course. It was difficult to forget his large presence, since he followed Melody around the room, and sat next to her, wherever she happened to be.

'I know—you'd like a brisk run around in the meadow,' she said, rubbing behind his ears. 'But we can't go out and leave Kristina, even though she's asleep, so you'll just have to settle down, old boy.'

And so shall I, she thought, wondering why she was in the grip of this restlessness.

As she sat, unsure of what to do with herself, she heard the doorbell ring and Lindi go to answer it, but she made no move, since she could not be expected to deal with anyone who called whilst Eva was out.

A few moments later, the lounge door opened, and Dieter von Rheinhof entered.

There was really no cause for surprise, since he called at any odd time when he happened to be passing, but she wondered why he stayed, when only she was there to receive him.

'Hallo,' she said, steadily enough, trying not to think of the moment the day before when she had turned and fled from him in the street. 'Didn't Lindi tell you—Frau Schulz is out, and Kristina is asleep.'

'She did, but since she assured me that the English *fraulein* was not busy, I told her I would come in for a few minutes,' he said gravely. 'Do you mind if I do?'

'Of course not,' she said. 'It's not my place to tell you that you are always welcome here. I'm sure you know it.'

'Yes?' His smile was faintly quizzical. 'I know it. But am I welcome to *you*, I wonder?'

She got up, and walked nervously to the bell Eva always rang for Lindi.

'Shall I ask for some coffee?'

'If you wish. But what I should really like is for us to be very English, and have afternoon tea.'

'Tea?' Melody, arrested in the moment of being about to press the bell, swung round to see if he was serious and not teasing her. It came to her that she, too, would love a cup of tea, for which, at times, all the coffee in the world was no substitute! 'Do you think Frau Schulz has any?'

'I'm sure she must have. Eva makes a point of being short of nothing her family or guests might require. It's a point of honour with her,' he said. 'But would you trust Lindi to make it?'

'Not for one moment!' Melody said fervently, and as their eyes met, felt her lips mirror his smile. 'If you'll excuse me for a moment, I shall do it myself.'

She went to the kitchen, followed faithfully by Siegfried, who sat outside the door, this being one room he was forbidden to enter. Sure enough, she found a packet of very good tea, and a china teapot in which to make it. Triumphantly, she carried the tray back into the lounge, and set it down on the onyx-topped table.

'I hope that is to your satisfaction, Herr Professor,'

she could not resist saying, with deliberate primness, as she poured carefully.

'Miss Cameron, I could not have been served better in a tea shop in Tunbridge Wells,' he responded in like manner, and Melody exclaimed.

'Good heavens! Whatever made you pick on Tunbridge Wells?'

'I have no idea, except that it sounds archetypally English,' he said. Then, irresistibly, both of them were laughing, companionable again, and she had almost forgotten the constraint she had felt when he first arrived.

When they had finished with the tea Melody, still not used to summoning servants to perform small tasks, took the tray into the kitchen. On her return, she noted that the room had suddenly grown darker. The sun had disappeared, and there were grey clouds scudding across the sky. With the changeability of mountain weather, rain was on the way.

Dieter was standing by the piano. Not seated at it, just standing, idly picking out the theme of a Mozart symphony with one hand, as if it were something he did almost unconsciously, whilst thinking of something else. With the same easy negligence, he brought the other hand into play, bringing in the harmony, and Melody suddenly envied him this ability which he appeared to take so casually for granted.

'I wish I could do that,' she said, the words slipping out without her having ordained that they should, a wistful note in her voice.

He stopped playing and looked at her across the room, and the austere lines of his face assumed a tenderness which was quite new to her.

'But it is nothing,' he said. 'Something I have done

from childhood. You never learned music? No, of course, in the circumstances of your upbringing you would not have had the chance.' She ached from the rush of understanding in his voice. 'It is not too late, you know, even now.'

Melody shook herself, trying to dispel the current that flowed between them.

'I probably would not have been any good at it,' she said practically. She switched on a lamp, as if the mere act of lighting up the room would bring her sharply back to her senses. 'Goodness, how dark it's getting! It will be raining any minute. I do hope you haven't far to drive.'

'Melody,' he said, cutting through her nervous chatter, and she stopped, remained still where she stood, unable to move as he left the piano and came towards her. 'I believe I caused you some distress yesterday. If so, then I apologise.'

Melody was instantly ready to meet him half way, so that she could, hopefully, forget the incident altogether.

'You weren't to know I would behave like an idiot,' she said warmly. 'I should have realised you were not serious and responded in kind. I'm . . . not very sophisticated, I'm afraid.'

'I am beginning to understand that,' he said. 'If you were, you would not so readily give me the benefit of the doubt, and assume I spoke in jest.'

She looked up, her eyes flooded with questions she dared not ask, and he said,

'The most serious matters may often be broached under the guise of banter, and desires we dare not admit to may masquerade as something more innocuous. I'm sorry if that's a touch Freudian for you.'

She blushed a little, gave a small nervous laugh, and said, 'Well, you should know,' aware that the current was still flowing, more strongly than ever, and that if she did not make a move to break it, very soon she would be in his arms, and all the firm promises she had made to herself would be as dust. Knowing that, she stood, unmoving, and it was he who turned away, leaving her full of an aching regret.

'Shall we agree to forget the whole thing?' he asked lightly, and she gulped and said, 'Yes, of course. Willingly,' wishing it could be accomplished as easily as that.

Mercifully for her, the sound of a car coming up the drive interrupted them, and Eva came into the room in a cloud of perfume, lightly shrugging off a fox fur jacket.

'Dieter—how nice. Does Kristina know you are here?'

'No, she's sleeping, and I did not wish to disturb her,' he said, 'but Melody has very properly acted as hostess, and we have just taken afternoon tea, English style.'

Eva grimaced.

'That's a pleasure I rarely have the chance to indulge in as Hugo hates the stuff, and refused to drink it even when we were in England,' she said. 'Why did it not occur to me to permit myself this small enjoyment whilst Melody is here?' She smiled graciously at them both. 'I think I shall just go up and look in on Kristina.'

'I'll do that, Frau Schulz,' Melody said quickly, but Eva forestalled her, insisting that she would go, and Melody could not help thinking that Eva had jumped at the chance to put her in the wrong, once again. Here you are, her attitude implied, chatting and drinking tea with my daughter's fiancé, but don't disturb yourself, *I* shall go up and see if the poor child is awake. Had she been awake, the bell connecting her room with the living quarters would have been ringing long ago, Melody had no doubt.

'I am afraid,' said Dieter, 'that I have just added

another job to your schedule. The reason Eva never drinks tea is not because Hugo does not like it, but because she has had no one to make it for her to her satisfaction. That someone has now been found.'

Melody laughed.

'That's all right, I don't mind,' she said. 'It's not as if I am ever overworked here, the way one often is on a hospital ward.'

'No—but here you are virtually always on call, whereas in the hospital, your hours would have been clearly defined,' he said.

'That's true, but many of my duties are by no means unpleasant. This morning, for example, Kristina and I went swimming.'

'You did?' His face registered immediate interest. 'Tell me, how did it go?'

'The actual swimming went very well. I think the exercise will strengthen her leg muscles, and she certainly enjoyed it.' Her expression clouded as she recalled the scene in the restaurant, and she found herself telling him about it, deriving reassurance from his quietly attentive manner.

'I know the Becker family,' he said. 'Klaus is a very well set up young man, who will eventually inherit his father's business. And a pleasant, thoroughly likeable person too. I agree with you that it is bad for Kristina to cut herself off from her friends. She should see more of people like young Klaus, people who are lively and yet dependable. It would not hurt for her to let him take her out now and again.

Melody's eyes opened very wide, and she studied his face closely. He was quite serious she saw, and perfectly untroubled by the notion of Kristina being escorted by Klaus.

'You wouldn't mind?' she asked.

'Mind? Why should I mind? It would do her good and that's what we all want, myself included,' he answered promptly.

Privately, Melody thought that this European sophistication went a little too far, but it was not for her to say so. Not for her, either, to repeat what Kristina had told her about her feelings for Dieter, and the difference she expected their eventual marriage to make to her life.

Hesitantly, she said,

'Do you mind if I ask your opinion on a professional basis? You are close to Kristina, and you are the only person I know who could possibly give me an answer.'

'Go ahead,' he said quietly.

'Very well. *I* think there is nothing preventing Kristina's recovery but herself. She has simply told herself that it's impossible, and refuses to try. Is that how you read the situation, or am I wildly off course?'

'You are asking me if the trouble is not physical, but psychological, is that it?' he prompted.

'Something like that. Tell me if you think I am talking nonsense.'

'Far from it,' he said. 'I would say you have made a fairly accurate diagnosis.'

Melody frowned.

'Then, if that is the case, can't *you* help her?' she asked.

He smiled.

'Not without her consent. And that she will not give,' he informed her, gravely.

'But I should have thought that if anyone could persuade her, it would be you.'

'Then you have overestimated my influence,' he said. 'I have suggested that she should come up to the outpatient clinic we have, and let us try to help her. She told me in no uncertain terms that because she could not walk, I was not to deduce that she was crazy.' He gave a wry smile. 'I told her it wasn't quite like that. I know we specialists tend to see everything in terms of our own speciality, but physical illness is bound up with the mind more often than many would like to believe. However, she would have none of it.'

'She is under twenty-one. Her parents could overrule her refusal, for her own sake,' Melody pointed out.

'Can you honestly see Eva consenting to that? And in any event, it would not help. If Kristina were seriously mentally ill, then the question of her co-operation would not be so crucial, and we could set it aside. Of course, we sometimes have to treat patients who are not capable of understanding or agreeing with their treatment. But in Kristina's case that does not apply. She has to *want* to be cured to be prepared to work with us. Do you understand?'

'I think so,' Melody said. 'Thank you for explaining it to me.'

'It was nothing. Your interest is laudable. You take your work seriously, and I like that.' He paused. 'If you are truly interested in *my* work, and I think you are, I should be pleased to have you visit the hospital. I trust you will take that invitation in the spirit in which it is intended, and not think I am making improper suggestions to you.'

She flushed.

'I assure you I shall not go off at a tangent again. Thank you very much, I should like to come. May I bring Kristina with me?'

A slow smile spread over his face.

'Up until now, wild horses have been unable to drag

her anywhere in the vicinity. But if *you* decide to visit us, I think that might just provide the spur.'

Watching him go, Melody had to fight to repress a feeling of bitterness. She had made the suggestion in order to set the girl he loved on the road to recovery, believing that if Kristina once visited the hospital, she would realise there was nothing to fear there and consent to treatment. Since the idea had been hers, why did it hurt that he had so readily agreed to use her as bait?

Kristina was enraged to discover that Dieter had been and gone whilst she was sleeping, and her rage fell squarely on Melody.

'Why didn't you wake me? You know I would have wanted to see him.'

'I know you were exhausted when we got home, and I wouldn't be much of a nurse if I put what you wanted before what was best for you,' Melody retorted.

'Oh, Melody, don't be so irritatingly virtuous! Haven't you ever been in love?'

'No, I told you I haven't. Even so, I don't see why half an hour of our afternoon is so vital. The main thing is to get you well, then you and Dieter can spend the rest of your lives together.' She winced a little as she said these words. Again, it hurt.

'Humph!' Kristina was only slightly mollified. 'It couldn't be that you let me sleep on in order that you could have a little tête-à-tête? What did you talk about, in my absence?'

'You, mostly,' she replied, truthfully. 'You could call it primarily a professional discussion. Kristina, why don't you attend Dieter's clinic? He seems to think he could help you, if you would only let him.'

The golden eyes were stormy and suspicious.

'So *you* think I am round the twist as well, do you? There's nothing wrong with my brain, Melody. It's functioning as well, now, as it ever did. I fell off a horse and injured my *spine*, that's why I can't walk.'

'Well, I'm no expert on psychiatry, but as I understand it, mind and body are closely interrelated, and your mind could be telling your legs that it's hopeless, and no use trying. That message could be corrected, through psychotherapy, but only if you go along with it.'

Kristina pulled a face.

'I can see you've been talking to Dieter. You're beginning to sound just like him.'

'Dieter is a very eminent specialist, Kristina. He knows what he is talking about. And surely it's worth a try.'

The other girl sighed.

'You've worked in the medical world for some time, Melody. You must know that Dieter cannot personally take me as a patient—it would not be ethical. And I'm not going to be sent up there and handed over to one of his side-kicks. Now let's stop arguing about it. It's wearing me out,' she said emphatically.

Melody shrugged nonchalantly.

'Oh, very well. It isn't my fault if you've got a bee in your bonnet about mental illness and the treatment of it,' she said. 'But I have no such inhibitions. Dieter has invited me to go and have a look around his hospital, and I fully intend taking up the invitation. I don't suppose you will want to come along,' she added slyly.

Kristina said nothing, for the moment, but her golden eyes narrowed as she looked at Melody. The English girl had the impression that she might just have won a minor victory, but it was not one in which, on her own account, she could take much pleasure.

CHAPTER SEVEN

As it happened, Kristina sat tight-lipped and silently resentful all the while during the drive to the hospital. She managed a smile for Dieter when he arrived to pick them up having taken precious time off work for the purpose of their visit, but to Melody she had scarcely spoken a word since breakfast.

Right up until the previous evening, she had maintained stubbornly that she would not go, and only in the morning, when Melody went to her bedroom to help her bath and dress, did she say grudgingly,

'All right, I'll come. But don't think I'm not aware of what you and Dieter have cooked up between you, and the answer is still "no".'

'That's up to you, Kristina,' Melody said equably, as she went through to run the bath. 'For my own part, I'm interested to see the hospital. I am a nurse, after all.'

She guessed it had cost Kristina a great deal to back down from her refusal, and only the thought of another girl—any girl—spending the morning in the company of Dieter von Rheinhof, had made it impossible for her to remain adamant.

Dieter himself was as calm and relaxed as ever, ignoring Kristina's smouldering resentment as if it did not exist. Melody wished she too could disregard the unpleasant atmosphere it caused. She gazed out of the window and tried to concentrate on the view.

The valley broadened out here, and gentle, pastoral countryside contrasted strongly with the splendour of

the mountains beyond. They drove for some time, and
then turned off up a long drive which led to high,
imposing gates. These opened soundlessly and closed
behind them, then they continued up the drive, with
pleasant, wooded parkland on either side, until they
came in sight of a spreading complex of low, modern
buildings, landscaped in lovely gardens.

'This is a psychiatric hospital?' Melody's laugh was
incredulous.

'Of course it is, Melody. There is a perimeter fence,'
Kristina said pointedly.

'So there is,' Dieter agreed, unperturbed, 'but the
ground are extensive, and it is not immediately obvious.
Some of my professional rivals like to insinuate that I am
running a holiday camp, because we have tennis courts
and a gymnasium, and try to make the place look
attractive. Depressing surroundings are no part of my
treatment. We want our patients to take a step towards
finding themselves, we do not want to alienate them
further.'

He got out and opened the door at her side, and
between them he and Melody got the wheelchair from
the boot, fixed it up, and installed Kristina in it.

A man weeding a nearby flower bed strolled up to
them and involved the Director of the Institute in a
prolonged discussion on various horticultural methods,
before returning to his task.

'You're certainly on familiar terms with your staff,
even the gardeners,' Melody observed, trying to trans-
pose a similar scene to the hospital where she had
worked, and failing utterly.

'I hope so, but that happened to be one of the patients,' he told her, smiling. A moment later, a young
man in cords and sweater hurried out of the main

building. By now, Melody was beyond being surprised when he was introduced as Dr Strauss.

'He didn't seem like a doctor,' she said doubtfully, after he left them.

'Because he did not wear a white coat, perhaps?' Dieter teased her gently. 'I only insist on uniform where it is strictly necessary. My staff do not walk around wearing distinguishing marks of the "you patient—me doctor" variety. Confused?' he asked, looking down into her face, which was full of bewildered interest. 'You'll get used to it.'

He devoted most of the morning to showing them around, and Melody was struck continually by the sur-roundings and the atmosphere, totally unlike any in-stitution for the mentally ill that she had ever seen or imagined. The common-rooms were airy and tastefully furnished; all manner of therapy was in progress, from painting and pottery in a specially-equipped craft work-shop, to exercise in the gymnasium, and squash and tennis on the courts. A drama group was engrossed in eager discussion, and the food being prepared in the gleaming kitchens would have been no disgrace to a resort hotel.

'Very impressive,' said Kristina, with a devilish gleam in her eyes. 'But you have shown us all the pleasant bits, Dieter. What about the rest?'

'You mean the padded cells and strait-jackets?' he said humorously. 'I am sorry to disappoint you, *lieb-chen*, but we have moved out of the nineteenth-century. Modern psychiatric practice is not like that, and very few of my patients need restraining. We do have some strapping orderlies for the odd occasion which may arise,' he added, with a suggestion of a twinkle in his own eyes.

He had the air of a man who was secure in his roots, and utterly fulfilled in his work, and Melody gave a small, involuntary sigh of something like envy. With a percipience which startled her, he said,

'It isn't all roses, Melody. Psychiatry is an exacting and often frustrating branch of medicine, although, more than any other, it allows the practitioner to express his own philosophy of life. And again, much of my work nowadays is administrative, to say nothing of lecturing, teaching—and in any odd, spare moments I have, usually at night, I'm writing up an account of my own approach to the treatment of mental illness, and how it differs from traditional methods.'

Melody glanced at Kristina's face, but it evinced only a blank uninterest. Nonetheless, she asked,

'Do you think you could explain to me, fairly simply, how it does differ?'

'I think so. In a nutshell, I am trying to establish here a therapeutic community, in which treatment is not measured only in actual time and physical attention given by the doctor, but in the total relationship of staff and patients, and everything that takes place in their environment. In which patients are encouraged to take as much responsibility for themselves as is possible, and in which staff have to reconsider the conventional etiquette of their training in favour of something less structured, based more on involvement and response.'

'It sounds almost revolutionary,' Melody observed.

'Well, in a way, although I am far from being the only one working along these lines. Others are doing something similar, so I am not a pioneer, maybe only a bit of a maverick. You see—you can regard mental illness as an organic problem, and treat it with drugs, or electro-convulsive therapy, or you can simply sit and do traditional Freudian analysis. And whilst all these methods have their place, I don't believe any one has a monopoly of rightness. My priority is the emotional climate in which treatment is carried out.'

Melody was thoughtful.

'The emotional climate? I always imagined a psychoanalyst as someone detached and remote.'

He laughed.

'Sitting on an exalted plane, somewhere above his patients, passing judgment like God? There are some who answer to that description, but I don't see my patients as malfunctioning organisms in need of adjustment. They are people, and I believe in involvement, in a spontaneous and open response, in genuine interaction between patient and therapist. Refusal to be oneself, to accept oneself, is at the root of so many of the problems I see. Does it help if I indulge in the same self-alienating behaviour I am trying to undo?'

Melody thought of the aloofness, the sudden withdrawal into an inner sanctum which she had sensed quite often in her dealings with him, and it occurred to her that this was a facet of his private life, not his professional one. Did one, then, have to be a patient to evoke an open and spontaneous response from Dieter von Rheinhof, or was there, after all, a way to reach the man behind the deep reserve?

They lunched in the pleasant dining-room, where several of the younger male members of staff made no secret of the fact that their day was considerably enlivened by the visit of the two girls. But obvious, also, was the immense respect all of them held for their medical director. In a place such as this, far more than in an institution run on more rigid, heirarchical lines, Melody could see that the personality and experience of the man at the top was of paramount importance. The structure may have appeared to be looser, more democratic, but it was held together as a coherent whole by the sure hand of Dieter von Rheinhof.

It had been a fascinating and informative experience for Melody, and when he had driven them home, she thanked him sincerely for taking the time and trouble to entertain them. But if the main purpose had been to introduce Kristina gently to the idea of Heiligenkreuz, she was not sure if it had been served at all.

As soon as they were alone, the smile she had forced herself to maintain in Dieter's presence was instantly wiped off her face, and she said coldly,

'I hadn't exactly expected the trip to be a bundle of fun, but neither had I envisaged having to sit like a stuffed dummy whilst you talked shop with Dieter.'

'You didn't have to do any such thing,' Melody pointed out. 'It was all couched in layman's language, and you could have joined in at any time. Aren't you interested in your future husband's profession?'

'It's a side of him I'd rather know as little as possible about,' Kristina said decisively. 'To be honest, the subject gives me the shudders.'

'That's rather a mediaeval reaction, don't you think? We've come a long way from Bedlam, as you saw this morning. It's going to be a strange marriage if you shut yourself away from what is, after all, the major part of his life.'

'When we are married, *I* intend to be the major part of my husband's life,' Kristina stated emphatically. 'Would you settle for second place, Melody? If so, then you *are* a mouse.'

'No, just a realist,' Melody grinned. 'I don't think I'd

set myself up in competition with Dieter's work if I were in your place.'

Kristina stretched her arms sinuously above her head, and her smile was not altogether pleasant.

'But you are not in my place,' she said tauntingly. 'Nor are you likely to be.'

Spring had come to the mountains and valleys of the Salzkammergut, with a fervour which declared that there was no going back. The sun was warm and strong, the air alive with birdsong, and the hillsides blossomed with a profusion of jewel-like Alpine flowers Melody had never seen before. Eva had put her patio furniture out on the large sun balcony, and Hugo had made arrangements to have the pool cleaned out, ready for the summer.

One such morning, when Melody took Siegfried for his walk—another of the tasks which seemed to have allotted themselves regularly to her—the dog was of a mind to go further than he usually did, and she followed him up the meadow until only the roof of the house was visible, far below. She had let him off the leash, and he was running back and forth with an explosion of pent-up energy, as if spring had got into his blood, too.

Melody sat down on the grass and let him take his time. He was a very large dog, and needed more exercise than he usually got, she thought. Kristina did not require her at the moment, and she was content to sit gazing down the hillside at the lake and the town, toylike at this distance, nestling by its shore.

'Good morning.'

She had not heard Dieter's footsteps approaching over the soft grass, and told herself it was only the unexpectedness of his presence which made her heart jump.

'Hello. Where did you come from?'

'Up there.' He pointed up the hillside. 'I saw you from a bend in the road, parked the car and walked down. It's such a lovely morning, and you looked so carefree, I could not resist joining you.'

He sat down at her side, seemingly unconcerned that the grass might mark his conservatively elegant dark suit.

'You were on your way to visit us? Kristina will be pleased to see you.'

'A brief visit only, I'm afraid. I am on my way to Salzburg. Some business first, and then I am to take my mother to lunch.'

'Your mother lives in Salzburg?'

'She does now. We have a rather draughty old *schloss*, up in the mountains, which is inhabited only by care-takers who keep it tidy and show the occasional tourist around. My mother prefers her centrally-heated ground floor apartment, close to the shops and amenities, and I suppose one can't blame her for that.'

'You have a castle? I'm impressed.' Melody wondered if he would ever take Kristina to live in the draughty *schloss*. She could not imagine the comfort-loving girl enjoying that, even if she had regained the use of her legs. On the other hand, she did have a strong romantic streak, and perhaps would appreciate being carried off to a castle by the man she loved. Again, that twinge of pain-regret gripped Melody, and again she banished it.

He laughed.

'It's miles from anywhere, inconvenient and lacking in creature comforts. My mother thinks I should maintain the family tradition by living in it, and I am constantly

trying to explain to her that if I did, it would be impossible for me to practise my profession. I expect we shall
re-fight this battle once more, today, in a very genteel
manner, of course. She's a very strong personality, my
mother, refined and cultured, with the resilience of iron
beneath the surface.'

'But you obviously win this particular battle, nonetheless,' she pointed out.

'That's because I am at least as determined as she is,
and I believe she knows this, and respects it,' he said.
'She never did understand the impulse which drew me
into psychiatry, but she accepts that it is the pivotal point
of my life, like it or not.'

Melody had a sudden, fierce intimation of how totally
different his life and background were from hers. He was
the end product of a long and proud tradition, secure in
the knowledge of who he was. Respected in his work,
and utterly dedicated to it, he still wore his learning
lightly, as if it were no more than his due. Whereas she
did not even have a name that was her own, stood
entirely alone in the world, and felt that what little she
had gained could at any time be pulled from under her
feet.

And yet, each time he visited the house—and there
had been several occasions since the afternoon they had
been alone—she felt anew the force of the attraction
flowing between them. She tried to tell herself it was
only in her imagination, tried to avoid his eyes, and to
limit direct conversation between them, but still the
feeling would not go away. Was anyone else aware of it,
she wondered? Fervently, she hoped not. It would not
do for Kristina's alert senses to pick up any such vibrations, and it had seemed to her that the only way to
prevent this was to keep on convincing herself that it was

all nonsense, and that she must stop being fanciful.

She must have sighed, without realising it, for he said, 'You looked so content with the world, when I saw you from the car. I hope it is not I who have clouded your vision of it.'

She turned to him impulsively.

'Oh no—you must not think that,' she said.

'Must I not? Sometimes you appear troubled, as if you have worries none of us can know of, and I feel a great need to alleviate your fears,' he told her.

'That's the psychiatrist in you, I expect,' she said.

'No. It is the man in me,' he corrected. 'You are very appealing, Melody. Generous and sincere, and yet there is a quality almost of wistfulness.' The long, sensitive fingers lightly touched her cheek, and he leaned forward and kissed her, very gently, on the mouth.

It was at the same time unexpected and utterly inevitable, and it was this sense of predetermination which held Melody spellbound, so that instead of drawing away, she found herself returning the kiss, and experiencing a sweetness, a wild joy that was new to her. And then it seemed that they had been moving towards this moment for so long that nothing could prevent it; she was in his arms in the long, scented grass, her hands rippling ecstatically through the shining thatch of his hair, and all her body alive with its response to him. She had never been kissed like this, tenderly, but with such knowing thoroughness, and she knew that in those few moments, he had overturned her life.

He drew away from her, just a little, but continued to look down into her face. Her hands had ruffled the usually immaculate hair, and the distinguished man of medicine looked suddenly much younger. She was beyond the veil of smiling, detached reserve he pre-

sented to the world, and both of them were suspended
on a slender, shining thread of enchantment, fragile and
beautiful.

She reached up to touch his face, wonderingly, still
caught up in emotions so new to her that she only half
believed in them. But even as she did so his smile faded,
the veil came down once more, shutting her out, and the
thread was broken. He drew away from her touch, as if it
might burn him.

'I am sorry, Melody. I must ask you to believe that was
not my intention. Sometimes these things happen,
whether we mean them to or not.'

She sat up, too, and unable to bear the sudden cool-
ness in his voice, coming so swiftly after the warm
excitement of their embrace, she looked down wretchedly at the grass, still crushed by the imprint of their
bodies. He should not have kissed her, and she should
not have returned his kisses with such delight whilst the
girl he was to marry was sitting helplessly in her wheelchair.

'I am as much to blame as you were,' she said in a small
voice.

'No. You are young, and by your own admission an
innocent abroad. Your only crime was your freshness
and charm. I bear the responsibility. I should not have
treated you . . . as I might have treated a more experienced woman.'

Melody still could not look at him. That was all it had
meant to him, she thought bitterly, a moment's enjoyment, brought about by proximity and physical attraction. A brief tumble in the grass with a young and
impressionable girl, to lighten the burden of a life full of
personal and professional responsibility.

'And if I were older, and more worldy, it would have

been permissible to make love to me—is that what you are saying?' she asked, her voice taut and controlled.

'It might. Do I shock you? I am only a man, after all. Look at me, Melody,' he commanded authoritatively. Against her will, she raised her eyes to his, which were steady and unwavering.

Her own were full of a deep hurt. She had given her response in terms he could not have mistaken, and he had drawn back because he recognised the sincerity of her ardour, and knew it was not in her nature to cope with a brief affair, with no hope of a lasting relationship.

She knew he was right, but all her feminine instincts were crying out against what they felt as rejection. So strong was the impulse to reach out and touch him, to fold herself into his arms and turn that rejection around, that she found it impossible to say anything which would make sense. He was not, she saw clearly, going to allow her to use those methods of persuasion to override his scruples. So she simply looked at him, and saw the wonder she had almost grasped ebbing from her, whilst her whole being ached with the loss.

The moment was only bearable because Siegfried chose it to return from his wanderings about the meadow, and clamber all over Dieter, demonstrating his welcome.

'Goodness knows where he's been, he's made muddy paw marks all over your jacket,' Melody said shakily. 'Down, Siegfried! Don't be a pest.' She made ineffective attempts to brush off the mud with her hands, and he rounded on her, quite sharply, and said, 'Leave it, Melody. I have a clothes brush in the car,' as if he could not bear her to touch him.

Tears welled up behind her eyes, and she forced them back.

'I had better go,' she said. 'Please don't come to the house right now.'

'I would not dream of it. That insensitive I am not,' he told her. 'For goodness' sake, don't make a tragedy out of it. It was only a kiss, after all.'

Yes, only a kiss, Melody thought, as she stumbled off blindly down the hillside with Siegfried in tow. For him, it would soon be forgotten, and could he be blamed if she were a foolish girl who had fallen in love with him, simply because he had kissed her?

That was not strictly true, an inner voice admonished her, however dramatic it might sound. Love does not come into being so swiftly, out of a clear sky. Rather, she had been moving towards it, step by step, from their first meeting, through all their fraught moments and half-tender, half-painful exchanges. What had come to her today was simply the realisation of a state which already existed. She loved him.

But no matter how it had come about, it was by far the most foolish thing she could have allowed to happen. For now not only must she suffer the agonies of a love that could not be requited, she must also hide it from everyone, avoiding Eva's vigilant eyes and the sharp antennae of Kristina's intuition. She must hide it from Dieter, too. He knew, of course—how could he fail to know?—that she found him attractive, but for the sake of her own self-respect, if nothing else, he must not realise that her heart was already deeply involved. She must behave towards him in a manner which was cool but friendly, and keep out of his way as much as possible.

CHAPTER EIGHT

SHE wondered if he had diplomatically decided it would be a good thing if they did not meet again for a while, for he avoided the Schulz house for the next few days, until Kristina began to grumble again about his neglect of her.

'And that wretched Klaus Becker has been phoning up every day since we saw him in the restaurant,' she complained accusingly to Melody, as if this fact were entirely her fault. 'I've made it quite plain I don't want to speak to him.'

'I think you're a bit hard on him, Kristina,' Melody said mildly.

'Hard? Life *is* hard. At least, it is on me. Is it so hard for him if he fancies himself in love with me, and I won't speak to him? He has the full use of his limbs, and the world is full of girls,' Kristina said angrily. She saw only her own desires as legitimate in this respect, and had short shrift for anyone else's. 'Melody, I'm not comfortable. Can't you do something about this chair?'

She looked closely at the English girl as she busied herself adjusting the seat.

'You're a bit absent-minded lately, you know. You brought me apricot jam with my rolls this morning, and you know I hate it, and several times you haven't heard me when I've spoken to you. I'd say you were in love if I didn't know better,' she taunted. 'Or perhaps you are. We don't know who you meet on your days off, do we?'

'Oh, really!' Melody exclaimed, trying to force a smile.

111

'Why "oh really"? Come to think of it, we don't know very much about you at all, do we? Who knows what secrets are lurking in your past?' She spoke lightly, jokingly, but the golden eyes watched Melody with knowing intentness.

'I'm only twenty-two, you know,' she said. 'How much "past" do you imagine I've had? You've got a very busy imagination—or what's more likely, too much free time to occupy.'

'Yes? And how would you have me occupy it?' she demanded sarcastically. 'Come on, Melody! I'm agog to hear what exciting new therapy nurse has in mind.'

'Since you mention it,' Melody said patiently, 'you might enrol for a course. Art, for example. Some of your sketches are really good. Why don't we get a prospectus and see what's available locally?'

Kristina gave a short, bitter laugh.

'What, me? Go to school? In this contraption? Not a chance!' she said vehemently.

'People in wheelchairs do all manner of things, aside from sitting and feeling sorry for themselves,' Melody pointed out tartly. 'It's about time you took a leaf out of their book, Kristina!'

The girl propelled herself over to the window and deliberately turned until her stubborn, angry back presented itself to Melody. Melody shrugged, and made no attempt to mollify her. She had sown the seed—she could only wait and see if it happened to germinate.

She was out of the room when, a short while later, the doorbell rang, and from her bedroom window she saw Dieter von Rheinhof's dark, discreetly expensive car parked outside. Sometime, I shall have to face him, she told herself, so it might as well be now. She squared her shoulders, forced a politely disinterested smile to her lips, and went downstairs.

At the door to the lounge, she halted abruptly. Eva was standing with her back to the door, unaware of Melody's approach, as was Dieter, who was seated next to Kristina, with her hands in his. Her hair tumbled forward in a golden curtain of loose curls, and she was gripping his hands very tightly, crying softly.

'I can't stand this kind of life any longer!' she sobbed. 'How can I go on like this? And now Melody is being absolutely beastly to me—can't she see that it's bad enough to be like this, without being bullied and nagged!'

Melody saw the golden head slump onto the man's shoulder, and his arms go around her, comfortingly. She couldn't bear to watch any more, but before she turned and fled back up the stairs, she had the distinct impression that Kristina had seen her standing there.

Later that afternoon, Hugo Schulz returned home from his office, and almost immediately, Melody received a summons to go and see him.

Hugo had a studio on the top floor of the house, away from all the bustle of the household. It was quiet and spacious, furnished only with drawing boards and filing cabinets, a desk and two modernistic leather swivel chairs. Wide windows let in the pure light, and gave a feeling of vastness and calm. Often he brought work home and retreated here to get on with it, untouched by the emotions of his womenfolk.

He was pouring himself a drink when she entered, having knocked and been told to come in.

'So—you catch me with my guilty secret,' he smiled. 'Will you, then, join me in it?'

'I don't drink very much,' she said.

'I know you don't. But just a small sherry, perhaps? Do please sit down, Melody. This is not an inquisition, no matter what you may be thinking.'

She sat in one of the leather chairs, feeling rather nervous, and with a good idea of what was coming.

'I understand from Eva that Kristina was rather upset today,' he began, and she observed, with sympathy, that he was finding this interview at least as difficult as she was. 'Their account goes that you were unpleasant to her, but I'm inclined to accept that this may be an exaggeration.'

She swallowed and bit her lip.

'I have tried, on various occasions, to explain to Frau Schulz what I am endeavouring to do, but not surprisingly, she reacts like a mother, and does not like to see Kristina disturbed,' she said. 'But I think she needs to be disturbed and yes, bullied a little, if necessary, to jerk her out of this apathy and hopelessness which, I believe, is holding back her recovery. All the same, I did not mean to upset her seriously, and if I have, then I'm sorry.'

He said, 'Kristina tends to over-dramatise, and always has. I understand that, but I doubt if Eva sees through it. However, Dieter von Rheinhof certainly does, and he rang me a few minutes ago. We had a long talk, and his explanation of what you are trying to do was virtually the same as the one you have just given me.'

'That was thoughtful of him,' Melody said. 'He need not have troubled on my account.'

'Dieter is punctiliously fair and would never allow anyone to be indicted without a fair hearing,' Hugo observed. 'I might also tell you that Eva was all for having you pack your bags, but I think I have convinced her that would be a retrograde step, and I hope you will not do so. I believe I warned you it might be difficult, did I not?'

'You did indeed,' she agreed.

'Then will you stay, please, Melody?'

'I'll stay . . . so long as you feel I am needed,' she said. In a way, she was sorely tempted to leave, in spite of having nowhere to go, just to get away from Eva's recurrent hostility, and Kristina's deliberate subversion of her efforts—not to mention the pain of loving a man her conscience forbade her to encourage. But she was not going to turn and run simply because the going had become a little rough. Nor was she going to permit Kristina to give up, which was what would happen if she left and Eva took over again. This one I *will* help, she had vowed, and she was not about to admit defeat so easily.

So she endured the somewhat strained atmosphere of dinner that evening, and the unmistakable gleam of triumph in Kristina's eyes. If she derived some satisfaction from getting me into trouble with her parents, it was only, she told herself, because that Machiavellian intelligence had so little else to divert it.

The next day, she made a point of collecting as many brochures and leaflets about art courses as she possibly could, and, saying nothing, deliberately left them where Kristina would see them. The girl said nothing, but Melody noted with approval that they had all been thumbed over.

A few days later, Kristina remarked,

'Dieter is going to take me into Salzburg tomorrow. He seems to think it would be an idea if you came along, although I can't see why we should need you. I suppose it will give you an opportunity to see the place.'

Melody was not sure if she was pleased or aghast at the prospect. A day in his company would be at the same time delight and torture, she thought. For hours at a stretch she would have to hide her feelings, conceal her emotions, pretend that he meant nothing to her, and she knew it would be far from easy. She wondered why he had suggested taking her. He could easily have coped with Kristina alone, and Melody remembered wryly the old expression 'three's a crowd'. Kristina would have adored a whole day of monopolising his attention, and surely she had a right to that.

But since it had been arranged, and there was no getting out of it, she decided she might as well make the most of it. She dressed smartly, but unpretentiously in a simple navy blue suit with white accessories and, since they were going to the city, put on make-up to give her a touch of sophistication.

Kristina's dress and jacket were vivid pink, and her hair tumbled loose over her slim shoulders.

'Aren't we a pretty pair?' she exclaimed mockingly, when Dieter arrived to collect them. 'I must say, Melody, a bit of make-up does wonders for you. You should wear it more often.'

'You look charming, both of you,' he agreed, with impeccable diplomacy. 'My reputation will be enhanced no end by being seen escorting not one, but two personable young women.'

Eva fussed around Kristina as she settled into the front passenger seat.

'You will take care of her . . . but what am I saying, of course you will.' Melody, folding up the wheelchair, heard Eva murmur to him, taking him on one side. 'I feel safer with her in your hands than I would with anyone else.'

'That's good of you, considering the circumstances,' he replied gravely.

Eva laid a carefully groomed hand on his arm.

'Ah, Dieter, you could not be held responsible for that,' she said, smiling urbanely. 'It gives me immense relief and confidence to know that you will always have Kristina's welfare at heart.'

Melody could not help wondering exactly what lay behind this little exchange of words. Considering the circumstances. What circumstances? And what was it she said he could not be held responsible for, whilst her tone of voice indicated that she obviously did just that?

'Here,' he said, appearing suddenly at her elbow whilst she was still lost in thought. 'Let me help you with that.'

'I can manage,' she muttered ungraciously, struggling with the chair in spite of her professed ability to cope.

'No doubt. But two pairs of hands can manage better,' he insisted, and between them, if was folded and stacked into the boot.

As she slid into the back seat, Melody heard Eva say,

'You will be seeing the Baroness, I presume? Give her my regards.'

'Yes, we shall be having lunch with my mother,' he confirmed.

The Baroness? Dieter's *mother*? Lunch with a Baroness, Melody thought, suddenly apprehensive. He had never told her the family was titled—but then, why should he have? Maybe that was just another of the things he took for granted.

Kristina chattered continuously for most of the journey, but her talk was calculated to exclude Melody from the conversation as much as possible. You are here purely in your capacity as nurse, that exclusion said, bluntly enough. Dieter made a point of drawing Melody's attention to any interesting features they passed, giving her an encapsulated history of a particular church, or remarking on an especially scenic vista, of which there were many. She replied with polite interest, but chose deliberately to remain quiet much of the time, concentrating on the beauty of the countryside through which they were travelling.

But on her first glimpse of the city of Salzburg, lying like a jewel in its splendid setting of green hills, her exclamation of pleasure was genuine, and could not be held back. The old and the newer parts of the city were neatly divided by the Salzach river flowing between them, and it was the mediaeval character of the old city—its towers, spires, cupolas and beautiful squares, its narrow lanes full of little old houses, struggling up the hill towards the castle of Hohensalzburg high above—which entranced Melody the moment she set eyes on it. Whatever difficulties the day ahead might hold she was infinitely glad she had come, and seen this ravishing place.

Taking turns to push the wheelchair, they wandered the narrow streets, admiring the innumerable architectural delights they came upon at every corner—almost an embarrassment of riches.

'Trinity Church,' Kristina said, as they turned into Makart Square, and since she was not an architect's daughter for nothing, added loftily, 'the frescoes are by Fischer von Erlach. Come on, Dieter, I suppose we are obliged to show Melody the Geburtshaus—the place where Mozart was born—no matter that you and I have seen it many times.'

'That is a shrine to which no music lover can return too often,' he laughed. 'After that, we shall relax for a while in the Mirabell gardens, before going to my mother's apartment.'

Baroness von Rheinhof lived in a gracious baroque house converted into apartments, off a delightful small square with a fountain at its centre. Her rooms were furnished almost entirely with antiques, not from any period in particular, but an amazing mixture of several. It said much for the owner's taste that these varied styles had intermarried in such a manner as to live amicably together. It said also that Dieter's mother was a determined individualist who chose what she liked, for no other reason beyond its personal appeal to her.

This frail-looking, extremely slender woman, with neat, silver hair, still managed to betray, with the shrewdness of her eyes and the patrician uprightness of her bearing, something of the steeliness of character her son had said she possessed. Only the strongest of wills would oppose her and survive the conflict, Melody thought.

'Kristina, child, how are you?' She surveyed the slim figure of the girl in the wheelchair with something of her son's compassionate but discerning scrutiny.

'As you see, Baroness, I am much the same as when you last saw me,' Kristina remarked, with a small shrug of the shoulders.

'Regrettable,' was the older woman's sole comment on this fact. Compassion Kristina might receive from Dieter's mother, but not the overflowing, sentimental pity Eva lavished on her, and the difference was not simply because this was not her own child. The woman who had now turned her perceptive attention upon Melody lived by a different code, she suspected, and sentiment was not its prime rule.

'And this must be the young lady you told me about,

Dieter,' she observed. 'The one with the unusual name.'

'Melody.' She took the thin hand extended to her, with a feeling she ought to curtsey, so regal was the other's manner. Then she smiled, and her face, in animation, was like his. Melody relaxed a little.

'*Jawohl*. Melody,' she repeated. 'Well, do come in all of you, don't hover in the doorway giving my neighbours something to gossip about.'

Lunch was served by a swift-footed, middle-aged maid, in a pleasant dining-room overlooking a small, paved courtyard, bright with tubs of spring flowers. From across the square, the bell of an old church clock punctuated the quarter hours with its chimes. The ambience was one of restrained dignity, elegance and quiet. Kristina's restless, pushful personality seemed confined and ill at ease in this almost old-world atmosphere, although she chatted brightly enough, and answered questions about her family.

Melody was quiet as she ate her Wiener Schnitzel and green salad, and drank dry white wine from the tall, green-stemmed glass in front of her. She scarcely knew her hostess well enough to initiate conversation, and Kristina, who had not wanted her along, was busy pretending she was not there. Which left Dieter, at whom she hardly dared look, for fear her emotions would be revealed in her eyes for all to see.

'We have been showing Melody a few of the sights of Salzburg,' he told his mother, refilling everyone's glass with more wine.

'And you have stunned her into silence with its magnificence, no doubt,' the Baroness said percipiently.

Melody laughed nervously.

'It is rather too much to absorb all at once,' she admitted. 'So many architectural treasures, so much

history and beauty compressed into so small a space—
and the most stupendous site.'

'The best view is from the Hohensalzburg—the castle,' said the Baroness, delicately omitting to mention
the obvious fact that they could hardly have pushed the
wheelchair up there. 'It is a hard climb. I do not mind
confessing to you that it is a good many years since I saw
Salzburg from that vantage point.'

She poured the coffee which her maid had just
brought to the table.

'And how are you going to pass the afternoon? More
sightseeing?'

Kristina stifled a groan.

'I hope not. I'm supposed to take a rest in the afternoon,' she pointed out, somewhat perversely, since she
chafed against the rest when at home, but was now
insisting upon it when she could have escaped its imposi-
tion for one day. 'Melody will just have to do without
seeing any more of Salzburg,' she added, with a kind of
grim satisfaction.

In her own home, she was quite accustomed to making
blunt statements such as this, secure in the knowledge
that no one would take exception to them. But the
Baroness was under no obligation to do the same, and
her eyebrows rose in slight disapproval.

'Really, dear, that's a little selfish, don't you think?'
she reproved mildly. 'Of course you must have your rest,
and so, incidentally, must I, so we shall be company for
one another. But we must not deprive Melody of taking
the opportunity, whilst you are not requiring her services. All this is new to her.'

She turned to her son, who was regarding her with
affectionate amusement, as if he read her mind all too
well.

'Dieter, why do you not take Melody up to the castle?' she suggested. 'You lead far too sedentary a life, and the exercise will do you good.'

'Nonsense, Mother. I ride and play tennis, and I ski in winter. I assure you, I'm perfectly fit. All the same, I shall be pleased to show Melody around.'

'Really, I can quite easily find my own way,' she protested. 'There's no need to trouble.'

'It's no trouble. Finish your coffee, and come along.'

It was difficult to ignore Kristina's sulky glare burning into her back as she left the apartment—she could feel the intensity of its venom. She wished the Baroness had not suggested he accompany her, wished he had not so firmly acceded to the plan. Kristina would be temperamental and difficult for the rest of the day, she knew, and Melody would suffer for every minute she deprived her of his presence.

But it would have been even more difficult not to enjoy the exhilarating climb up the steep little streets to the impressive fortress of Hohensalzburg. And she had no need of the official guide with Dieter to show her round.

'It was originally built by Archbishop Gehbard in 1077, and of course has been added to since,' he told her. 'You can well imagine that it was virtually impregnable in earlier times. The archbishops were the creators and rulers of Salzburg, both religious and temporal—the most famous was Wolf Dietrich, a great patron of the arts, who built the Cathedral and the Mirabell Palace.'

They studied the marble reliefs in the chapel, the princes' chambers, and admired the amazing view over the city and its environs from the Reckturm tower.

'You could spend a lifetime here, and still find things to wonder at,' she said.

'That is true,' he agreed. 'I have spent most of my life here, apart from the years I lived in America, and although I do travel quite a lot, attending conferences and so on, my home and my life's work are here.'

'It must be truly wonderful,' Melody said wistfully, 'to have such direction and purpose in life.'

'*You* must have a sense of purpose, too, Melody. Can't you remember the day when you decided to be a nurse, when you said, *that's* what I want to do?'

'Yes,' she said slowly, 'I suppose I can. But I seem, momentarily, to have lost my way.'

'Sometimes, when we feel that, it is only that we have set our foot on a new path—which may prove to be the right one.'

He drew her through an archway set in a high wall, and she found herself in a delightful, tree-shaded *Biergarten*, totally unexpected and hidden from the street.

'We have had a long climb on a warm day. I think we have earned a glass of wine,' he observed.

Seated at a table under the trees, Melody could hear music spilling out from the cafe's interior, where a quartet of string musicians were playing.

'It's Mozart!' she exclaimed.

'What else?' he asked. '*Eine Kleine Nachtmusik*, to be exact. Music is a living presence in this city, which is another reason why I love it. Just wait until August when the Festival is upon us! Of course, it becomes very crowded, and my mother complains of the cars choking the streets, but for a whole month, music is king.'

The sun was warm, the wine light and refreshing, and the music soared, taking Melody with it. She knew they should be thinking of going back to the apartment, but she could not help savouring guiltily the bittersweet joy of this short time with him. Stolen moments, that was all they were. He wasn't hers, and could not be.

'You are pensive again, Melody.' She looked up to find him regarding her with that close, penetrating gaze she found so unnerving. 'What is it?'

'Nothing, only . . . I think, perhaps, we should be going back.'

'You are anxious not to be alone with me. You know, Melody, you are not exactly inflating my ego,' he told her, with just a touch of mockery.

Recalling what had taken place the last time they had been alone together, Melody thought this was distinctly unfair.

'I don't think your ego needs any help from me!' she retorted.

'Why not?' His voice was slightly ironic. 'Because I have a certain kudos on account of my work? Because my family have lived here since the sixteenth-century, and my mother is a Baroness? Do you think that makes any difference to *me*, to my inner feelings?'

He had touched her on a raw spot, and she would have jumped from her seat if he had not laid a firm hand on her arm and held her still.

'No, Melody, do not always run away. It is time you confronted these feelings of inadequacy in yourself, and recognised that everyone else shares them, to some extent.'

'Even you?' The sarcasm in her voice was a defence against the emotions he had reawakened in her, and he combatted it swiftly.

'Even I, for all you think I am arrogant and detached, am not immune. Pain and loneliness and longing are not yours alone. And nor is guilt, which I divine, although you have not told me so, seems to trouble you more than anything.'

She looked down again.

'You divine too much. I am not one of your patients.'

'Indeed, no.' He laughed softly. 'It is fortunate you are not. For you, I prescribe a therapy I would never suggest for them.'

And now she did get to her feet, swiftly and nervously. The only other customers had left the garden, and they were screened from the café by the bright young greenery of the trees. She leaned back weakly against the gnarled trunk of one of them as he stood up, pushing aside his chair. Moving close to her, he slid his hand behind her neck, running it up through the thickness of her hair.

'No, Dieter . . . it isn't fair!' she protested. 'You must not . . . you can't!'

'Can't I? We shall see,' he challenged implacably. 'Right now, for example, I am going to kiss you. So forbid me—if you can.'

If you can. He had flung a gauntlet at her feet, and she was powerless to pick it up. High above, the fortress of Hohensalzburg frowned down on them as if in disapproval, but the garden was full of bright sunshine and birdsong, and music, and she did not protest any further as his mouth found hers. He held her lightly, so that at any moment she could have broken free, had she wanted to, and in giving her that choice, which of her own free will she declined to make, he proved his point beyond contention. After a long moment, when she was almost molten with bliss, he drew away, quite deliberately, regarding her with a faintly triumphant smile.

'It is not a good idea to tell me I "cannot" do something,' he said. 'You might do well to remember that. Now I had better go in search of the waiter. He appears to be too busy listening to the music to come for his money.'

Melody stood in the garden awaiting his return. Tears of shame had sprung to her eyes, and she brushed them away impatiently. For what purpose had he demonstrated to her, so explicitly, the strength of her own desires? Was it merely a need to exert his will over hers? He did not love her, and it was unkind of him to play games with her in this manner.

She was so wrapped up in her own misery that she did not hear him return. The first she knew of it, he was standing beside her, touching her cheek with his fingers, lightly, comfortingly, as if he were not the one who had caused the slight dampness he discovered there.

'Tears?' he said. 'Was it then, so awful an experience, to be kissed? I had not thought so from your reaction at the time, I must confess.'

'I am not crying!' Melody said, through clenched teeth. 'All right, so you kissed me, and I didn't dislike it—I am human, you know!'

'Extremely so,' he agreed, producing a clean white handkerchief from his pocket, which she accepted, in spite of her insistence that she was not in tears. Dabbing ineffectually at her face, she said,

'If your male pride objects to being dictated to, then may I ask you, please, not to kiss me again, at any time?'

He looked at her thoughtfully for a moment, and then shrugged.

'Very well. I shall accede to your quite reasonable request,' he said, equably. 'But I am not going to apologise to you for something we both found enjoyable. If you have finished with my handkerchief, shall we make our way back to the apartment?'

They stepped out into the street again, and continued

their descent from Hohensalzburg. By the time they reached the Residenzplatz, dominated by the magnificent baroque cathedral, Melody had regained a measure of self-control, and was able to listen calmly enough as he pointed out the arcades connecting the cathedral with the Chapter Square, in the centre of which stood the Kapitelschwemme, a fountain which had once served as a watering place for the archbishop's horses. She was grateful to him for his precise, dry, guide-book manner, deliberately devoid of emotion, which helped her to assume once more a correct and composed demeanour.

'What a splendidly sonorous language German is,' she observed. 'Full of great, long, self-important words, like "Kapitelschwemme".'

'Isn't it?' he agreed. 'Many of them are only series of words strung together, you know, but it does help to make the meaning exact and unmistakable. It is the language of psychoanalysis, in which the great giants, Freud and Jung, wrote. But also the language of romance and philosophy . . . hence Goethe, Schiller, Hegel, Nietzsche . . . I won't go on, the list is endless.'

As they walked the narrow streets back to the Baroness's apartment, Melody, aware that she might not have another chance to speak to him privately, said,

'Thank you for taking me up to the castle . . . and indeed, for bringing me to Salzburg. It's a wonderful city, and your mother is an amazing lady, so gracious and so kind.'

'There is no need to thank me. I wanted you to see Salzburg, and to meet my mother,' he said, with a gravity which perplexed and disturbed her.

'I'm grateful, although I feel I should not have come. Kristina would much rather have had your company exclusively—and you hers,' she said awkwardly.

In the shadow of the church, looking across the small square with the fountain, he paused.

'Melody.'

There was something indefinable in his voice which made her look up at him, expectantly.

'Yes?'

'I was not speaking academically when I said I understood about feelings of guilt and responsibility. You may not know this, but Kristina was not alone when she suffered that riding accident which left her so badly injured. She was with me.'

She continued to gaze up at him, understanding, now, the meaning of that brief conversation she had overheard between Eva and him that morning. Understanding, too, the complex web of emotion and circumstance which bound him to Kristina.

'I taught her to ride when she was little more than a child,' he said, 'so who knew better than I her abilities and her limitations? She watched me take a high fence, on this particular occasion, and decided she wanted to try it. I advised her not to. She has always been headstrong and self-willed, but until then had never gone directly against my wishes. This time, for some reason, she decided to prove she was her own mistress. She rushed the jump before I could prevent her.'

'Dieter, you must know that it was not your fault,' Melody said, wryly aware, with some part of her mind, that she was a fine one to be talking about self-exoneration. 'It was pure accident, and you could not have done anything to stop it.'

'Of course I *know* that, Melody,' he said. 'I did not cause it, could not prevent it, and it might have happened at any time, when I was elsewhere, with the same result.' He shrugged. 'However, our faculties of reason and logic are often prey to other forces, beyond our control, and so I do not entirely convince myself.'

The chime of the bell from the little church rang in Melody's ears as they crossed the square, but it did not drown the echo of his words, reverberating in her head, and she was assailed by a heavy sense of doom and hopelessness.

CHAPTER NINE

'THAT certainly took you long enough,' Kristina said petulantly, on their arrival. 'I hope you have seen everything now, Melody, because I think we should be starting back. My mother will worry if I am away from home too long.'

'I shall telephone and assure her you are on your way,' the Baroness promised soothingly. 'I hope you will have made some definite improvement by the next time we meet.'

She kissed Kristina briefly on the cheek, and turned to her son. 'I suppose it is no use whatsoever my admonishing you for working through the night, you will still go right ahead and do it,' she said, with affectionate resignation.

'I suppose I shall, Mother, but I will endeavour not to do it too often,' he promised.

'You see how much filial respect one gets from one's sons after they have become men?' she appealed to Melody, but the love and pride in her eyes rendered the complaint meaningless. '*Auf Wiedersehen*, my dear. I do hope we shall meet again.'

Melody had been fully expecting Kristina to sulk on the return journey, but she showed her displeasure by resolutely conversing all the time in German, something she rarely did in Melody's company. Then she lapsed into silence, and the golden head drooped against Dieter's shoulder as he drove. Relegated to the back seat, Melody leaned back and half-closed her eyes, trying not

130

to let these minor irritations worry her. In spite of the occasional remarks addressed to her by Dieter, she felt—as Kristina fully intended that she should—very much the odd one out in this party. Of what consequence was it that he had kissed her so passionately in the garden? The girl at his side, leaning so proprietorially against him, was the one who would share his life.

Eva was vastly relieved to have her daughter back under her roof again, and fussed over her as if she had been on a world tour, not simply a car trip of a few miles.

'You'll stay for tea, or coffee, perhaps?' she asked Dieter, but he declined politely.

'Thank you, no. I must be getting back. I have a lot of work to do.'

'I understand. You work too hard, of course.'

'So my mother has just been telling me, also,' he replied, with a smile. 'But today was a pleasure, and pleasure, unfortunately, has to be paid for.'

His eyes met Melody's, briefly, but the expression in them remained the same, friendly but impersonal. Was it possible that this calm, restrained individual was the man who had shattered her senses so short a while ago? She could not help watching him through the window as he got into his car and drove away. She had asked him not to kiss her again, and he had said he would not do so, but at least half of her did not wish him to keep that promise.

'You look tired, dear,' Eva said to her daughter.

'I am,' Kristina complained, 'even though I was very good, and had my rest. I'm not used to being out for so long. And the Baroness is kind enough in her way, but not terribly sympathetic. Anyone would think I enjoyed being like this!'

'Of course you don't, *liebchen*, and I'm sure she

doesn't think so. She's a proud, aristocratic old lady, and one just has to accept her as she is.'

Kristina grunted.

'I had plenty of practice, today. Dieter and Melody left me at the apartment whilst they went up the Hohensalzburg, and they were gone for simply ages.'

'It wasn't really such a long time,' Melody protested, 'considering how stiff a climb it is.' She blotted out the memory of the time in the garden, which had, anyhow, added no more than a few minutes to the total.

'It certainly seemed like it!' Kristina retorted, with the injured air of a child who had been left behind whilst the grown-ups were out enjoying themselves. 'And another thing, Melody, now I come to think of it—how long has Dieter been addressing you as "*du*"?'

Melody did not falter under that interrogative stare, but she could not hide the tell-tale colour which enlivened her pale skin.

'I can't exactly say. We usually talk in English, so it doesn't arise. But I've known him for a while now, it hardly seems necessary to be formal.'

Oh, for the blessed anonymity of the English language, where the familiar form went out of usage centuries ago, and everyone was addressed as 'you', regardless of the degree of intimacy of the relationship, Melody thought.

Kristina's smile was far from pleasant, but she did not dispute the point. Having made it in Eva's hearing was sufficient for her.

'I think I shall lie on my bed and read for a while,' she said. 'And some tea would be a good idea, Melody.'

After she had taken Kristina upstairs and made her comfortable, Melody went down to the kitchen and began to make the tea. Whilst she was waiting for the automatic kettle to boil, Eva drifted in, with apparent vagueness—but Melody had learned that nothing Eva Schulz did was truly purposeless.

However, she did not appear angry or displeased, but smiled and asked, 'Did you enjoy Salzburg?'

'Oh yes, indeed, I thought it was beautiful,' Melody said sincerely.

'I think you have not travelled much?' It was half statement, half question.

'Very little. Until I came here, I had never been out of England.'

'I thought so. Everything is very new and exciting, no? And of course, it is very pleasant to see these wonderful sights in the company of someone like Dieter, who knows the area so well, and is, besides, an assured and sophisticated escort.'

Melody began to have an intimation of what this was all about. The subtlety of Eva's approach had temporarily relaxed her guard, but now she was alert, her senses tingling with danger.

'It's always best to be shown around by someone knowledgeable,' she agreed, as equably as possible.

'Quite so,' Eva said smoothly. 'Dieter von Rheinhof is a most attractive, cultured and interesting man, wouldn't you say? Not the kind of man a girl meets every day of her life. I must admit, if I were twenty, and single, I would find him so, and I don't blame you, Melody, for being a little . . . how shall we say . . . captivated?'

The kettle switched itself off. Glad to have something to do, Melody poured the water into the teapot. When she turned back to Eva again, she was in command of herself.

'Dieter is everything you say he is, but I think both you and Kristina are over-reacting a little,' she said calmly.

'The Baroness merely suggested that he should show me around the castle, which he agreed to do.'

'Well, *natürlich*, being the gentleman he is, he would hardly refuse, would he?' Eva smiled. 'You are a nice girl, Melody, but not very worldly, I think, and you could be forgiven for reading more into that than was intended.'

Melody fetched the milk from the fridge, and poured it into the silver jug which Eva kept for that purpose.

'I assure you, Frau Schulz, that there is no danger of my doing that,' she said, truthfully enough. She had woven no romantic dreams out of the fact that Dieter had kissed her. Captivated, indeed! she thought ruefully. She wondered what Eva would say if she told her that she was deeply in love with Dieter von Rheinhof, what she would say if she knew how this refined and cultured man had deliberately and ruthlessly shown Melody the extent of her own involvement!

'I am relieved to hear it,' Eva said smoothly. 'I would hate you to imagine yourself into a situation where you might be hurt. That would not do at all. Because he is going to marry Kristina, you know.'

'Yes, I do know, Frau Schulz. Kristina has told me,' Melody replied steadily.

'Well, of course, we have always known that they would marry, as soon as Kristina was old enough,' Eva continued. 'She needs a mature and intelligent man, strong enough to cope with her moods, and especially now this will be the best possible match for her. But it is difficult for both of them, at the moment, whilst she is not well enough to be out and about in his company, as she would be in normal circumstances. The situation is complicated enough. I am asking you not to make it more so.'

She picked up the cup of tea Melody had poured for her, and left the room. A dignified and glorious exit. Melody felt demeaned, as if her love for Dieter had been written off as the infatuation of an innocent girl out of her depth, fascinated by a man and a culture beyond her normal experience.

'I was beginning to think you had forgotten,' Kristina commented, when she finally took up the tea tray. 'I hope the tea isn't cold.'

'It won't be cold.' Melody set the tray on the bedside table and poured out a cup. 'I'll be up to help you get ready for dinner in a while. I expect you feel like taking a bath, first.'

'I most certainly do. But no exercises, please. Today has been tiring enough.'

She looked at Melody from where she sat, propped up against the pillows, her hair a bright tumble against the palest blue. Her eyes held a wicked gleam.

'*Mutti* has been warning you off, I expect,' she said bluntly.

Since the girl had most expertly manipulated her mother into doing just that, Melody thought she should not be surprised that her ploy had succeeded.

'We had a bit of a talk,' she admitted.

'She seems,' Kristina said innocently, 'to have got it into her head that you've been giving Dieter the eye.'

'I wonder how she managed to get hold of that idea,' Melody said drily.

'I can't imagine. Because you wouldn't do anything so despicable, would you?' Kristina said softly. 'When you know how things stand, it would be mean to take advantage of a girl who is in a wheelchair, wouldn't it?'

Melody sighed. Suddenly, she was bone-weary, and wished she need have nothing more to do with the

complicated emotional situation in which she seemed to
have landed herself.

'I think it's high time you stopped using that chair as a
refuge, and rejoined the human race,' she countered
quietly.

Kristina banged the cup down on the tray, so hard that
the fragile handle broke off in her hand and tea spilled all
over the tray.

'Now see what you've made me do!' she glowered.
'That cup belongs to one of *Mutti*'s best china sets, and
she'll be furious! Take it away. I don't want any more
tea.'

She may well be furious, but with me, not with you,
Melody thought. She picked up the tray, and as she
reached the bedroom door Kristina called softly,
'Melody.'

She paused. 'Yes?'

'Dieter is not for you.'

'I never thought he was, Kristina.'

With unsteady footsteps and hands that shook, she
succeeded, somehow, in getting the tray back to the
kitchen without breaking any more of Eva's china.

It had been a long and emotionally taxing day, and
Melody was surprised to find that in the morning, there
were no visible signs of trauma in the household. Eva
came down to breakfast as smilingly polite and cool as
ever. Max was late, as usual, and his father waited
impatiently to give him a lift to school. And Kristina,
when Melody took up her breakfast, was in one of her
vital and energetic moods, poring over the leaflets
Melody had left in her room not so many days before.

She patted the edge of the bed.

'Sit down a minute, Melody,' she invited, and Melody

perched on the edge watching Kristina spreading jam on her rolls, all her movements betraying her restless impatience.

'I'm bored!' she said, with the air of one giving out an official pronunciamento.

'But of course you are,' Melody said, all her sympathy for the girl coming back in a rush. 'It's perfectly natural for you to be so. You lived a full and energetic life before, and have all your wits about you.'

Kristina turned the leaflet she had been reading towards Melody and spread the page.

'I was looking at this. It's a course of lectures at the local college of art.'

'"The Baroque Experience in Art and Architecture",' Melody read. 'Sounds like just the thing for you. Shall we go along today and get you enrolled?'

'You don't waste any time, do you?'

'No. Strike whilst the iron is hot, that's me.'

'Then I hope you realise that if I attend these lectures, you'll be the one who has to take me there and bring me home again.'

'That's all right. I'll even sit through them with you, if you like, although I doubt if I could tell baroque from gothic, unless it was explained to me in words of one syllable.'

Kristina's glance was shrewd.

'That won't be necessary, and don't pretend to be dense. You aren't fooling me, not for one minute,' she said. 'In fact, I have a feeling that there's a lot more to you than meets the eye.'

'As there is to most of us,' Melody said levelly.

'Not all. Some people are all surface, all show, without very much underneath. Others are the iceberg type, with two-thirds hidden. Dieter is like that,' she reflected.

'You think you know him, but lo and behold, there's another layer, and yet another. It can be very irritating.'

Melody smiled, concealing a small twinge of pain near her heart.

'He puts a lot of himself into his work, and so there's a side of him that only his patients, and perhaps his colleagues, truly know,' she said.

'And another side, which only his wife will know,' Kristina pointed out with satisfaction. 'Do you think you will ever marry, Melody, or will you turn into a dried-up old spinster, all starchy and unfulfilled?'

'I couldn't really say.' Kristina was in a provocative frame of mind, but Melody refused to be provoked. 'In any event, marriage is only one road to fulfillment. There are others.'

'For some, perhaps. But if *you* don't have children of your own, you will never be part of a family, will you?'

This was the unkindest jibe of all, because it was so patently true that there could be no arguing against it. Kristina had so much, in spite of her present disability— a loving family, a secure and affluent background, and eventual marriage to a man she adored. Her words were like a dash of cold water in Melody's face, reminding her that she had very little in comparison.

She squared her shoulders resolutely. She had her health, and her ability to work—it would have to be enough. She had known love, too, even though it was a forbidden, fugitive emotion which she must hide and suppress, still it was there, and in her own heart she could not deny it. So she turned away Kristina's taunts by ignoring them, pretending that they had not hurt her.

'I think we had better get you dressed if we're going to the college so you can enrol for the course,' she said evenly. 'Now, what would you like to wear?'

Kristina took such an avid interest in the course that Melody wondered, with cautious excitement, if this might be the turning point for her. Innumerable books were borrowed from the library, and ordered from publishers' lists, and she spent hours reading and making notes. Two afternoons a week, Melody ferried her back and forth to the college, where, for virtually the first time since her accident, she ventured amongst other people, and found herself accepted on equal terms as just another student, whose mental faculties were by no means impaired by her relative immobility. There was talk, only tentative, of a full-time course, beginning in September after the summer recess. Melody hoped this might be the incentive which finally persuaded the girl to make a real effort to walk again.

Meanwhile, they continued with the exercises and the swimming. It was now warm enough to use the Schulzes' outdoor pool on good days, and to spend a good deal of time outside in the open air. Both girls began to develop healthy tans from the hours spent in the sunshine.

One afternoon, whilst Melody was waiting in the college cafeteria for Kristina's class to end, she glanced up, and quite unexpectedly found Dieter at her side.

'May I?' he said, slipping into the seat next to her. 'I came only to say goodbye. I am going to Geneva tomorrow, to meet a colleague there, then on to London, and over to New York for a few days for an international symposium.'

'It all sounds very exciting,' Melody said, trying to ignore the thumping of her own heart.

'Not really. I would sooner be here, attending to my everyday business, but one has to be prepared to explain and defend one's ideas from time to time. Can I get you another coffee, whilst we wait for Kristina? I am going to have one myself.'

'Please,' she said, not because she really wanted more coffee, but because it would give her something to do with her hands, and conceal some of the nervousness she felt in his presence.

She had seen little of him since the day they went to Salzburg, and that little had been in the Schulz household, with all the family present. He had made no attempt to see her alone, and there was not the slighest intimation in his manner towards her of what had passed between them on that memorable day. She had asked him to leave her alone, and he had respected her wishes to the letter. Perhaps he realised that although he found her passingly attractive, flirting with her was really not worth the trouble it would bring about were Kristina to have any inkling of it. Or it could have been that it was so unimportant to him that it was already gone from his mind. He had so many other more pressing matters with which to concern himself. Why should he worry about what had been, at best, the impulse of the moment to kiss a girl who obviously wanted him to do so, in spite of her denials?

She glanced at her watch as he returned with the coffee.

'Kristina should be out in five minutes, but they have a very enthusiastic teacher and sometimes they run a little late,' she said.

'No matter. I shall wait. I think this is a marvellous project for Kristina, and you deserve all praise for getting her to do it.'

She flushed with pleasure.

'Thank you. But really I did very little, apart from leaving the brochures where she could see them. Kristina can't be pushed. She has to be nudged, ever so gently, so she thinks the idea is all hers. But I expect you know that,' she added, with a rush of embarrassment.

'I do now,' he said. 'Perhaps I should have known it sooner, but I was so used to bossing her around since she was a small girl, and I had the advantage of my extra years. I had not realised that the small girl was suddenly a woman, but no less wilful.'

'You are still blaming yourself,' she said.

'Up to a point, I always shall,' he replied. 'And you, Melody—are you still blaming yourself for whatever it was that went wrong, which has made you so wary and so hypercritical of yourself?'

She had not intended telling him about it. Indeed, she had thought she would keep it locked away inside her, and never tell anyone. But the tremendous force of sympathy which seemed to flow from him, enveloping her in a warm, healing tide of pure and disinterested concern, opened up a dark and fearful place in her emotions. And for the first time, she looked into that place without averting her gaze in dread, as if he took her by the hand and said, 'Look, now—it isn't so bad. Face what you fear, and having done so, it will never again have the same power to terrify you.'

And so she told him, quietly and unfalteringly, leaving nothing out, and he listened, without any change of expression, calm and accepting, and quite unshockable.

'There are two things here, as I see it,' he said, at length. 'One is that you *know*, beyond question, that you were innocent of any involvement with this man. It was, perhaps, unwise to become caught in the cross-currents between two people who were married, but you acted from the purest of motives—friendship.'

She nodded. 'I've learned that lesson, now. But could I have kept my distance, and let Liane flounder?'

'Being you, probably not,' he said.

She frowned. 'You said there were two things, Dieter. The other one . . . ?'

'You tell me, Melody,' he said quietly, his gaze probing. 'Spell it out, once and for all.'

She took a deep breath, aware that this seeming ruthlessness was in her own interest, and that, quite rightly, he was not going to let her off the hook.

'All right. I am afraid that she might have heard the rumours that were flying around, believed them, and crashed the car deliberately. And the worst of it is that I shall never know.'

'Exactly,' he said. 'For you, that *is* the worst of it. I cannot wave a magic wand and resolve this for you. On the balance of probabilities, I would say it was pure accident, but I think you know this, too. Your friend was close to alcoholism, and her husband should not have allowed her to drive, but people in this state can be cunningly adept at hiding it, and he probably had no idea how much she had had to drink over the whole day. From what you tell me, although she was clearly disturbed, I would not have thought she was suicidal. The drinking was more of a cry for help and attention. But I cannot be definite, nor can you, nor will you ever be. You must live with it, accept it, and begin to absolve yourself.'

His voice was quiet and his eyes steady. At no time had he offered her a panacea, in fact, he had categorically denied that one existed. So Melody could not have said why she felt such a lightening of the spirit. Not that anyone had lifted a burden from her shoulders in one miraculous movement, it was rather as if she had been shown a way in which she might carry it more easily, accepting its weight but no longer bowed down by it.

'Thank you,' she said impulsively and quite sincerely, a smile lighting her face.

'For what? I did nothing, for the most part I merely listened. *You* confronted your fears and took the first step towards overcoming them. You should be doubly pleased with yourself, both on account of that, and of what you are doing for Kristina. Our combined efforts failed to bring her to Heiligenkreuz, but this might prove to be the better therapy.'

'I hope so,' Melody said, still warm from the praise he had accorded her.

'Why? Is it simply a natural desire for Kristina to recover, or are you anxious to return to England and rejoin your Health Service when your patient no longer requires your services?'

The question, so wryly phrased, caught her by surprise, and without a definite answer.

'I don't know . . . I haven't really thought about it. Perhaps I shall do that, in the future. But for a long time the hospital was a cocoon for me, and having been forced out, I don't know that I'm eager immediately to crawl back in.'

'The bird has learned to use its wings,' he said softly. Was that mockery in his voice, or was it merely her imagination? 'You could always consider working for me.'

Melody jerked bolt upright.

'For you?' she said, astonished.

'Yes. You would need retraining first, of course, but you are a good nurse, and you have the right qualities.' He laughed. 'Do not look so aghast. You think I would be unspeakable to work for? I assure you I am a reasonable employer, and don't ask more from my staff than I am prepared to give myself.'

'Oh no . . . I'm sure you don't . . . that is . . .' Melody was flustered. Work for Dieter von Rheinhof? Become one of his staff, a dedicated member of his therapeutic community? She was sure that to work with him would be a tremendous experience, but there was another side to it, which made her doubt the wisdom of undertaking such a course of action. She would see him every day, speak to him, perhaps be closely involved with him in a working situation, and when he was married to Kristina and even more firmly unavailable than he was now, would she be strong enough, emotionally, to handle all this would mean to her? She had a feeling it would be better to put the whole of Europe between them. But how could she tell him she could not work with him because she loved him too much?

'I should have to think about it,' she prevaricated.

'Naturally,' he said. 'I don't want any hasty decisions. In fact, I should require you to be very sure. Ah, class must be out—here comes Kristina, now.'

Kristina, in a soft summer dress of mingled pinks and blues, her hair caught back with a ribbon, her face glowing with life and interest, propelled herself eagerly towards them in her wheelchair. Melody was struck anew by her vivid beauty.

'Here I am, Mel, get some coffee, I'm gasping!' she cried. 'Dieter—how lovely to see you, but what brings you here at this time of day?'

He took the hand she held out to him.

'As I have just been telling Melody, I came to say goodbye. I'm off to Geneva tomorrow, then to London and New York,' he told her, and she groaned, her elation evaporating visibly.

'You are always going away!' she moaned.

'It's a hazard of my profession, I'm afraid,' he said. 'But I always come back.'

'And I'm always afraid that you won't. One of those wretched planes might crash or something,' she said morosely.

Melody almost dropped the tray on which she was stacking the cups.

'Kristina!' she exclaimed, horrified.

He laughed.

'It's all right, Melody. I have to admit to having the same apprehension myself, but it hasn't happened yet, and one can't live in a box lined with cotton wool,' he said. He stood up, and took the tray out of her hands. She was sure he must have noticed that they were trembling.

Not five minutes before, she had decided it would be better for a continent to divide them from each other, and now she was shaking at the mere possibility that something untoward might befall him. What, then, of all the future years, when he could be ill, or hurt, could die, even, and she would not be there? When, by taking herself out of his life, she would have made a statement that it was none of her concern? When would it end, she wondered, bleakly, and how could she bear it?

CHAPTER TEN

'ALL this jetting around the world,' Kristina grumbled, as Melody drove them home.

'Well, since that isn't going to change, you'll have to get used to spending a certain amount of time alone,' Melody pointed out.

'Alone? Not I,' Kristina said vehemently. 'I won't be the kind of wife who sits meekly at home. I shall go with him.'

'In the wheelchair?' countered Melody. 'Yes, I know it can be done, but look at the difficulties. Airport terminals and hotels for the most part aren't geared towards the disabled. And what would you do whilst he was in conference—sit in your hotel room and wait?'

'All right!' Kristina snapped. 'You've made your point!'

'Have I? I keep making it all the time, but we don't seem to be getting any further forward. All the exercises have made your legs so much stronger, you're fitter in yourself, and I'm sure you could walk if you would only try.'

Kristina remained stubbornly silent, and Melody pressed on.

'Now there's this full-time course you're considering. It would be far easier for you if you were walking—and by September you could be.'

'Hobbling, you mean. On crutches.'

'To begin with, yes. But you would be surprised how quickly you would progress once you started. Think

146

about it. Before too long, you could dance, drive your car . . . and when you married, you could be a real wife, not just a semi-invalid.'

She tried to keep her voice even, concealing the pain this picture she was painting caused her, but glancing at Kristina, she saw real distress in the golden eyes.

'Don't!' she said hoarsely. 'Damn you, Melody, stop it! Give me some peace!'

Her anguish was so obviously not feigned, Melody subsided. She had somehow got to Kristina, in a way she had never succeeded in doing before, and she could see that behind the girl's beautiful mask was a kind of fear. If she could only find its roots, she would know what was preventing her patient's recovery. But it eluded her—just. She was like a child chasing a butterfly, which fluttered on to the next flower just as her hand reached out to touch it.

By the time they arrived home, Kristina's composure had returned, and she chatted animatedly to Eva about the class.

'It's remarkable,' Hugo said later to Melody, 'the difference in her since she started this course. It seems to have opened up the world for her again, and it's wonderful to see her enthusiastic about something. It was a brainwave on your part, Melody.'

Again she disclaimed any credit, but Hugo was insistent.

'No, really. It was your idea, and modest or not, you must not deny it. She's improving, mentally and physically, anyone can see that, and much of it is thanks to you. But we still have the same problem, don't we? She isn't on her feet, or showing any signs of being, and I wonder what will happen when she returns to the hospital for her next check-up.'

Melody frowned.

'When they see she's making no progress, they will probably want to admit her again.'

'Yes. That was what I was afraid you would say. She isn't going to like that. And Eva will go to pieces.' He frowned, too, in anticipation of his household disintegrating into chaos once more.

The days that followed were increasingly warm and sunny. Melody and Kristina lazed by the pool and occasionally took drives in the countryside, with a picnic hamper in the car. On her days off, Melody explored the villages of the Salzkammergut, travelling from one to another on the local buses. Having learned that the region had been so named owing to the salt that had been mined there since Roman times, she felt she should investigate this phenomenon, and duly went on a guided tour. Kitted up in regulation white overalls, she passed through mine shafts in a car running on rails, and crossed the salt lake by boat, after which strange, underground experience, she was relieved to emerge once more into the sunlight and the open air.

She went once again to Salzburg, aware that in one day she could hardly have brushed the surface of all there was to see. But it was full of memories. Along the narrow streets of the Altstadt, Dieter walked at her side; every corner seemed to mark a spot where they had paused to gaze at a church, a fountain or a house, and she could not bear to retrace their route to the Hohensalzburg, or visit again the tree-shaded *Biergarten*. The excursion was not a success, and she was glad to board the bus and return home.

She missed him, of course, but in a way there was a certain relief in knowing he would not, at any time, turn up at the house. She would not have to endure the agony of making polite conversation whilst her emotions were in turmoil. And yet, she counted the days secretly, as avidly as Kristina did, eager for the time when he would be safely back again.

One summer morning, she got up as usual, unknowing that a time bomb was ticking away in her life, measuring the seconds towards the time when it was due to explode.

It was an unexceptional day on the surface, no different from any other. Kristina had ordered some books on art from the bookshop in town, and the shop had telephoned to say the order was ready.

'Be an angel and fetch them for me, Mel,' she said. 'I don't feel like coming along. It's going to be hot, and I'd sooner sit by the pool. Take the car—it will be easier than going by bus.'

Since she was on an errand for Kristina Melody agreed, and set off. She drove with the window wound down to let in the fresh breeze, and her arms were bare and brown beneath the short cap sleeves of her light cotton dress.

She had difficulty in finding a parking place. The holiday season was just just coming into full swing and the little town was crowded with visitors, shopping, sailing on the lake, and thronging the tiny bathing beach. It was market day, too, and the main square was taken up with traders and their stalls. Melody finally squeezed into a vacant space and hurried along to the bookshop. She did not linger, knowing that Kristina would be avid for the books and that patience was not one of her chief attributes, but what with the trouble parking, and contending with the traffic, it took her far longer than she had expected.

A strange car was parked outside the house when she

returned, a car she did not recall having seen there before. It did not belong to any of Eva's regular visitors, and it wasn't the racy little convertible driven by Klaus Becker—who had twice visited since they met him in the restaurant, much to Kristina's annoyance.

But the fact of the car's being there was not in itself disturbing, and Melody picked up her pile of books and went indoors without any premonition of what was awaiting her.

She had not expected to find anyone in the lounge at all. At this time of day she had thought Eva and Kristina would be out on the sun terrace, drinking their mid-morning coffee. Certainly coffee had been served, the tray and cups were still on the onyx table. Both Eva and Kristina were there, the girl with a wild, excited glimmer in her eyes, her mother stiff-faced and correct. Between them, in one of the plush armchairs, sat none other than Nurse Laura Bailey.

She smiled, a little, secretive smile, as Melody entered.

'Hello, Melody. I was beginning to think I should have to leave without seeing you,' she said, as if it were entirely natural and not at all unexpected for her to be sitting in Eva's lounge.

'Laura! Whatever brings you here?' Melody exclaimed, too surprised to make a thorough job of concealing her dismay. She had thought to have left that part of her life behind her, and here was this girl who had helped stir up so much ill-feeling against her, come, like a ghost, to haunt her with it again. Her brain was spinning, and she could not immediately think what Laura was doing there. But instinctively, she realised that her presence boded no good.

'I'm on holiday—on a coach tour,' the other replied.

'We're staying in St Wolfgang tonight—you know, the *White Horse Inn* village. Tomorrow we shall be off again, on our way to Venice, but I felt I couldn't pass through without looking in on you, so I hired a car and drove up. I hope you don't mind,' she added sweetly. No one would have believed, from her manner, that she had resented Melody so fiercely because of her failure to get the job she had wanted.

'Well . . . that is, I'm just surprised, that's all,' she heard herself stammering. 'I never expected . . .' Still bemused, her heart hammering with apprehension, she remembered the pile of books she held in her arms, and took refuge in them.

'I brought your books, Kristina. I'm sorry it took so long, but there was hardly anywhere to park.'

Kristina had apparently lost all interest in the books she had been so eagerly awaiting.

'Oh, put them down on the table,' she said offhandedly. 'I'll look at them later.'

Laura Bailey stood up.

'Look at the time! I shall have to be off, I'm afraid,' she said, suddenly anxious to be gone. 'We're booked on a tour of the Salzkammergut after lunch, and I don't want to miss it. Thank you for the coffee, Frau Schulz. Sorry it was such a flying visit, Melody.'

'You're quite welcome, Miss Bailey,' Eva said, in her formal hostess's tone. Her smile was thin, and it froze as her eyes came to rest on Melody. 'Perhaps you would like to see your friend out to the car,' she suggested.

'Yes. Yes, of course.' Melody came to life, and still in a partial daze, walked with Laura down the drive to where she had left the car. She had no desire for conversation, and wished simply that the other girl would drive off and leave her in peace, but as she might have guessed, that was not to be.

'Nice place,' Laura observed, a gesture of her hand encompassing the house and its grounds, and all the surrounding grandeur of the mountains. 'Super house— very posh. They must have pots of money. You landed on your feet there, didn't you?'

Melody could not bring herself to reply, it was all too contrived and obvious, but Laura chatted on, regardless.

'And that girl—why, she's the image of Liane Garret! I almost passed out from shock when I saw her.'

'There is a certain facial resemblance,' Melody said stiffly.

'Oh, come on! She could be Liane's sister!' Her hand on the door handle of the car, Laura paused and looked curiously at Melody.

'You're wondering how I found out you were here? It wasn't difficult. We all knew you'd gone to work in Austria, and that Mrs Moore had fixed it up for you. You know how impossible it is for anything to remain secret in the hospital for very long. So when I knew I'd be passing through, I asked her for your address. Told her I was sorry for helping the rumours along, and wanted to put things right between us. The old dear believed that—but you don't have to,' she added softly. 'I don't so easily forgive anyone for standing in the way of what I want.'

Melody sighed.

'It's all so unnecessary, Laura, this antipathy. I had nothing against you, why take it so personally, because I got the job and you didn't? It happens all the time, and you know it. And I expect you're working on Orthopaedics now, anyway.'

'Well, you expect wrong!' Laura burst out fiercely. 'I put in for it when you left, but that old bag of a sister on there wouldn't have me. Still thinks there's nobody like you, Melody, in spite of everything. And they promoted a newly qualified SRN over my head.'

'I'm sorry,' Melody said awkwardly. In a way, she meant it sincerely enough. She did not think Laura Bailey was destined for a successful career in nursing. She might be competent enough, but somehow her personality was all wrong for this very exacting profession. But there was little to be gained from pointing this out to her. It was something she would have to find out for herself, and perhaps she was beginning to do so, although as yet she had not grasped the reason for her failures, and was still laying the blame at Melody's door.

'Sorry!' repeated Laura, vehemently. She got into the car, then wound down the window and looked up at Melody with a faint smirk of satisfaction. 'Not half as sorry as you are going to be!' she said.

Melody watched her reverse, turn, and drive off down the road. Only when the car was out of sight, did she turn and walk slowly back towards the house. All at once, she was conscious of a reluctance to go back inside that was almost fear, and it would have taken only a slight faltering of her nerve to send her running off in the direction the car had just taken.

Because Laura had not gone to the trouble of finding Melody's address and seeking her out merely to satisfy her curiosity. That might well have been part of it, but not all. Whatever she had said to Eva, whilst Melody was not present, the girl knew it would not be favourable to her. With the deepest foreboding she forced herself to face the result without hesitation.

Eva was alone in the lounge. She was standing near the window, quite still, obviously awaiting Melody's return. Her manner was impeccably controlled, but her expression was glacial and Melody shivered. She has never really liked me, she thought, never wanted me here in the first place, and never made me welcome. At best, she has only tolerated me. She closed the door quietly, and stood facing Eva, since it would have been inane to pretend that everything was normal, and that a showdown was not imminent.

'I have taken Kristina up to her room,' said Eva, 'because I thought it only right that what I have to say should be for your ears alone.'

She paused, sweeping Melody from head to toe with a look of icy contempt.

'I agreed to take you into this household, with some reluctance on my own part, on the advice of my daughter's doctors, and also because of my husband's persuasion,' she said. 'Your references were good, and I have no real complaint as to your competence as a nurse. But you came to us very much on trust, and it will not surprise you to hear that I feel that trust has been betrayed.'

'But it does surprise me,' Melody declared, stung into defending herself. 'I am a fully-qualified nurse, and I have done what you employed me to do to the best of my abilities. I don't know what Nurse Bailey has been saying to you, but . . .'

'Ah!' Eva pounced. 'So you admit, do you not, that there was something to be said, something you would have preferred us not to know? You must not blame your friend from England. When I suspect that something is amiss, and wish to know the truth, I can be very persistent.'

'Laura Bailey was never my friend,' Melody said bluntly.

'Those who know the truth are always feared by those who wish to conceal it,' Eva observed. 'Fraulein Bailey was, in fact, adamant in stating that the episode in question was not wholly your fault. An inexperienced girl, an older, married man, *nicht wahr*?'

'It wasn't like that,' Melody said despairingly. If only she had been there when Laura arrived. But then she would never have dared make such insinuations, cleverly allowing Eva to extract from her such information as she fully intended her to have.

'Then it was not true that the man's wife crashed the car, deliberately killing herself and him, because of his involvement with you?' Eva demanded coldly.

'No! That is . . . I don't know,' Melody floundered helplessly.

'So,' Eva pronounced coolly. 'Those are the facts, are they not? You will gain little by denying them. I can quite easily verify all this if I choose to do so.'

'The facts are that the car crashed, and they were killed,' Melody admitted. 'Whether it was deliberate, no one will ever know, and I was not, at any time, involved with James Garret. That is all I have to say.'

Eva's disbelief was written all too clearly on her proud features.

'That is all you have to say? Don't you think you owe us some form of explanation as to why you kept so quiet about all this, if you are as blameless as you claim? I must say, I'm surprised at Avril Moore, going along with such a cover-up.'

'*She* believed me, and she thought, as I do, that none of it had any relevance to my abilities as a nurse,' Melody cried.

'I happen to think differently,' Eva said coldly. 'Would I have employed you to look after my child, my only daughter, who means so much to me, had I known? Would I have entrusted her welfare to a . . . a Jezebel?'

Melody took a step back, recoiling from the virulence of the accusation.

'I am *not* a Jezebel, Frau Schulz!'

Eva's voice was suddenly soft, but it had a menacing sibilance that was more unnerving than her anger had been.

'You are certainly not what you have pretended to be, *Fraulein*. Right from the start there was something about you which I mistrusted. I knew you could not be quite the Miss Innocent you would have had us all believe you were. Your reaction when you saw Miss Bailey spoke for itself, and now, I think I have found your Achilles heel . . . men.'

The insinuation was so breathtakingly unwarranted that for a moment Melody could think of nothing sensible to say in her own defence. Nor did Eva give her any opportunity.

'Do not think I am unaware that right from the day you arrived here, you have had your eye on Dieter von Rheinhof. I guessed you travelled on the same place, and you very probably began angling for him then, if the truth were known!'

'That's not true!' Melody gasped. There was something so vulgar about this middle-aged woman demeaning herself with such an expression, that she was swept by a wave of distaste. 'I have never "angled" for him, at any time!'

Eva's carefully plucked brows arched inquiringly over her icy blue eyes.

'And you would deny any interest, I suppose?' she said. 'You do not find him in the least attractive? Come, *fraulein*, I too am a woman of the world!'

Melody stood dumbstruck. She could have bluffed it out and made a denial, but Eva, she knew, would not have believed her. Furthermore, she felt that to do so would in some way traduce her own integrity, which was now all that she had left. Everything she had told Eva had been the truth. To lie now, about this, would be to reduce that truth to a mockery.

For this, she saw clearly now, was her real crime. Eva was not really so incensed by the real or imagined misdemeanours in Melody's past. What she could not countenance was her interest in the man she herself had earmarked as her daughter's future husband, particularly if there were the remotest chance that interest might be reciprocated. And here, like a positive gift from heaven, came Nurse Laura Bailey, ready to put ammunition into Eva's hands.

The two women looked at each other for a few moments.

'So,' Eva said, eventually. She went over to the walnut escritoire in the corner, in which she kept her household accounts and writing materials, and Melody saw her scribbling something rapidly. When she crossed the room once more, it was discernible as a cheque, upon which the ink of Eva's signature had just dried.

'I think,' she said, 'that it would be better all round if you were to leave at once. Do not wait until my husband returns in the hope that you can talk him round to your point of view. You did that once before, but this time I am quite adamant, and Hugo will not fight me. This pays you up to date, I think.'

She saw Melody shake her head in unspoken refusal,

and a small smile curled her lips as she pressed the cheque into the girl's inert hand.

'Take it, *fraulein*. It is no more than you have earned, and you cannot, I think, afford to be too proud.'

Melody's head went up. Maybe she could not. So all right, the Schulzes had money and position, and she was simply a little English nurse, a nobody, without family or standing, penniless except for what she could earn herself. But she was not about to succumb to this indignity, no matter what. She let the cheque drop from her hand, and it fluttered slowly to the rich oriental carpet.

'Maybe not everyone can afford pride, Frau Schulz,' she said. 'But I, of all people, cannot afford to be without it.'

Eva gave a brief shrug. She did not insist.

'As you wish,' she said. 'I am going out for a short while now. When I return, I shall expect you to be out of the house. And I would ask you not to disturb Kristina further, or involve her in this. In fact, it would be better if you did not see her at all.'

'Not even to say goodbye?' Melody cried involuntarily.

'Consider it said,' Eva stated haughtily, and she swept from the room without a backward glance.

Still shaking a little, Melody went upstairs to her room, and with trembling, unsteady fingers, began to pack her clothes and personal possessions in her suitcase.

It had all happened so quickly. This morning had been the start of just another day, then Laura had turned up, with deliberately malicious intent. Eva had attacked her with a verbal savagery from which she was still reeling, and now, it seemed, her Austrian interlude was over. She no longer had a job, a home, or anywhere to go.

It did not seem as if she had any option other than to get herself to Salzburg, catch a plane, and return to England. She did not seriously consider Dieter's offer of a job. For one thing, as he had said, she would need more training if she intended to take him up on the offer, so it was not an immediate possibility. Besides which, there were all kinds of emotional reasons why it would not be a good thing for her to do. And Dieter was out of the country, anyhow. She could not even turn to him as a friend.

She was glad, at least, that she had told him her story, so he would not have to hear only the version Eva had so readily believed, as interpreted by Laura Bailey. He won't accept that, she thought, he's too fair, too balanced, and too experienced in the judgment of human nature.

Melody did not have a lot in the way of material possessions, and it did not take her long to pack, particularly since she hurried, anxious to be away before Eva returned. Forcefully, she clicked the suitcase shut, and took a last, regretful look around her pleasant room, and out of the window at the splendid view she had come to love. So much had happened to her since she first saw this room, she felt she was scarcely the same girl, but it was over now. Just another chapter which was almost closed.

Much against her inclinations, she had stood by Eva's instruction not to see Kristina, and had studiously avoided the interconnecting door between their rooms whilst she packed. But now, just as she was about to pick up her suitcase and go downstairs, the girl's familiar, demanding voice called out sharply,

'Melody? Are you still there?'

Melody stood perfectly still, not saying a word. If she

were quiet enough, Kristina might assume she had already left, and then she could creep silently down the stairs. However, Kristina was not so easily fooled.

'Melody!' she repeated impatiently. 'I know you're in there, because I heard you moving about. For goodness' sake, don't leave me in the dark like this! Tell me what's going on.'

It was beyond her to remain silent when Kristina was so obviously aware of her presence.

'Your mother will tell you,' she said wretchedly. 'I'm going now. Goodbye, Kristina.'

'Oh no you don't!' Kristina shouted, in furious frustration. 'Melody, that's not fair, sneaking off like that! You know I can't come after you!'

Melody had her hand on the doorknob, her suitcase gripped firmly in her other hand. Then there was a shuffling sound from the other room, and a sudden loud thud.

She dropped the suitcase on the floor and flew across the room, all Eva's injunctions forgotten as she reacted with the spontaneity of instinct, wrenching open the connecting door.

Kristina was sprawled on the floor, at least three feet from the bed, where, if the array of magazines were anything to go by, she had previously been lying. She grinned up, rakishly, at Melody.

'You see,' she said, 'I told you, you can't just walk out like that. Why, I might do myself a mischief.'

Melody went down on her knees and helped the girl to a sitting position.

'Are you hurt?' she asked, and Kristina shook her head.

'No, I'm all right.'

Melody surveyed the distance between the bed and

the place where both of them were now seated on the floor. Then she looked back at Kristina again, and the other girl smiled, reading her thoughts without difficulty.

'It's a fair old step for someone who can't walk, isn't it?' she agreed. 'More of a stumble than a step, really. And look what a mess I made of it.'

'What's significant is that you made it at all,' Melody said. 'Your own curiosity, and anger at your helplessness, gave you the impetus you needed.'

She lifted Kristina back on to the bed, and made her comfortable.

'*Now* will you believe me?' she said.

Kristina looked thoughtfully at her.

'Whether I believe you or not isn't relevant,' she said seriously. Then, abruptly changing the subject, she demanded, 'You are leaving, aren't you?'

Melody inclined her head.

'Your mother seems to think it will be best if I do.'

'I know. That girl let *Mutti* drag all that stuff out of her ever so cleverly, as if she really didn't want to tell her, but she didn't fool me. Did you really have an affair with your friend's husband?'

'No,' Melody said firmly, meeting the golden eyes without allowing her own gaze to falter. Kristina nodded.

'I believe you,' she said evenly. 'In a way, I shall be sorry to see you go, but all things considered, I think *Mutti* is right, it's probably for the best.'

It was quite unnecessary to ask for an explanation of this. Melody understood perfectly the underlying reason why both Eva and Kristina wished her to leave, so she did not comment on it.

'But I wish I were not leaving now, just as you are on

the verge of making some progress,' she said.

Kristina shook her head.

'That didn't happen,' she said. 'I did not make any attempt to get out of bed, and it's no use telling anyone I did. I shall deny it, it will be your word against mine, and who is going to believe you—especially now?'

Melody stared at her.

'This I don't believe,' she declared. 'Are you seriously telling me that now you *know* you've an excellent chance of walking again, you're not going to do your utmost to consolidate it?'

The lovely mouth twisted in a strange, bitter smile.

'And throw away my strongest weapon?' she said softly. 'I want to marry Dieter. He's a difficult man to be sure of, but we *shall* be married, because every time he looks at me, he is reminded of the circumstances in which I came to be this way.'

Melody sat down suddenly on the edge of the bed. Right from the beginning she had known that Kristina's inability to walk was not entirely dependent on physical factors, that she had convinced herself it could not be, and deliberately set her face against an attempt to improve her lot. Perhaps unconsciously at first, but now fully aware of what she was doing, she had decided that to keep this man at her side, to ensure that he was hers, she must lean on the sense of responsibility he felt on her account.

'Kristina, this is crazy,' she said. 'Not only because the longer you refuse to help yourself, the more you jeopardise your chances of full recovery, but because it's immoral. If Dieter loves you, he will marry you. Do you want it to be on account of a lingering guilt about your accident, rather than because he cares for you, and wants you for his wife?'

'Let's say I'd rather not take any chances,' Kristina answered, with a grim and quite implacable determination. 'All's fair in love and war, Melody!'

'But that isn't love!' Melody said adamantly. 'It's the worst case of emotional blackmail I ever heard!'

As Melody knew, to her cost, so often happened, Kristina's mood changed with alarming abruptness.

'I'm not interested in your opinion!' she cried, her eyes flashing angry sparks. 'You've tried your best to sabotage my plans from the moment you arrived here, but you are not going to get in my way any longer! So get out, and go back where you belong—wherever that might be!'

Melody stood up, went back into her own room, and closed the door quietly behind her. Then she picked up her suitcase and handbag, and without looking back went quickly down the stairs. All at once she was sickened—surfeited with the atmosphere of this house, with the ostentatious luxury which shouted that its owners must display their wealth; with the hothouse climate of Eva's intense and overindulgent affection for her daughter; but most of all, with Kristina and her overweening insistence that her will should triumph, her needs should be gratified at whatever cost.

In the hall, Siegfried stretched his long body, ambled over to her, and looked at her with anxious, enquiring eyes. Briefly, she bent and put her face next to his huge, gentle one, and he nuzzled her ear.

'I tried,' she whispered to him. 'I honestly tried. But there's nothing more that I can do here.'

CHAPTER ELEVEN

THE BUS deposited Melody in Salzburg, and she stood
for a moment, temporarily uncertain what to do. She
thought it might be rather pleasant to splash out on a taxi
to the airport, but another bus would be cheaper. Having allowed herself the luxury of refusing Eva's cheque,
she really should not indulge in unnecessary extrava-
gance. She had not needed to spend much of the salary
she had earned during the last few months, but what she
had banked would have to last her until she found
another job, and she had no way of knowing how long
that would take.

It occurred to her that she should first of all ascertain
whether there was a suitable flight today as, if none was
available, she would have to book into a hotel for the
night. She could have phoned from the Schulz house,
but she had been in too much of a hurry, at the last, to get
out of there. A quick visit to the tourist information
office assured her that there was a plane later that day,
and a convenient bus to get her to the airport, which left
her with time to spare for a meal and a final, nostalgic
walk around.

She wasn't really all that hungry. It was long past
lunch time and too early for dinner, so she contented
herself with coffee and cakes. She had intended making
use of the bureau de change facilities at the airport to
ensure that she had sufficient English money for her
arrival in London late in the evening. But having used up
the last of her loose notes and change on the fare to

Salzburg and the snack, she decided that she had better go along to the nearest bank and cash a cheque, or she would have nothing for the bus to the airport.

She was actually in the queue for the cashier when she realised that something was wrong. She could not find her cheque book. Rummaging anxiously through her handbag, she saw it was her turn, and she was holding up the queue.

'*Entschuldigung, bitte,*' she muttered, and stood to one side to let the queue proceed. She had begun to feel distinctly anxious. In the pocket where her cheque book, credit cards, documents and passport usually resided neatly together there was nothing. On a small table she emptied out the contents of her handbag to ensure she had not, just this once, slipped them into the wrong compartment. Make-up pochette, purse (empty), handkerchief, a folded up chiffon scarf . . . but no sign of the essential documents.

Piling everything back into her bag and picking up her suitcase, Melody sought the open air. Outside, she collapsed thankfully onto a bench, cold with horror, although the afternoon sun was warm. In her haste to get away she had left her most important possessions behind. She knew, now, exactly where they were. Changing handbags one day, she had omitted to transfer them, and they were in a small drawer in the dressing table of her former bedroom. She was alone in Salzburg, without money and without a passport. She could travel nowhere, stay nowhere.

'Oh, what an idiot I am!' she moaned, as myriad harebrained solutions rushed through her head, and were rejected. She could *not* face the thought of going meekly back and confessing she had left these vital things behind, encountering once more Eva's icy contempt, and Kristina's frustrated fury. She did not even have the money for the fare back. She considered telephoning and asking for her documents to be posted to her, but it would need to be a reverse charge call, for which she would have to ask Eva to pay, and she would still have no money to support her until they arrived. Every idea which came to her had a flaw in it. It seemed there was no way she could turn.

What did people do when they got themselves into difficulties abroad? They went to their country's representative, she supposed, and asked for help. If she found her way to the British consulate they might lend her money, but she would still have to go and fetch her passport.

Melody buried her bowed head in her hands, uncaring of the spectacle of despair she might present to anyone passing by, sunk in the deepest gloom and self-pity she had known in a long time. No one cared anyway, she thought, the self-reliance which had supported her throughout her solitary young life ebbing away. On a bench in this beautiful city surrounded by mountains, with the sun shining, and people hurrying past, intent on their own affairs, she reached, perhaps, the lowest point of her life, where there seemed to be not a glimmer of light on her horizon. She had been summarily dismissed from her job, was without money or friends, and the man she loved was forever beyond her reach. What was the point in picking herself up, only to struggle on a little further?

It lasted only a few minutes, then she sat up sharply, muttering, 'Pull yourself together, girl!' There had to be a way back from the depths, there always was, and she would find it. Just as there had to be an answer to her present dilemma, if only she could think clearly enough to see it.

And then it came to her. She was not entirely alone in this city—there was someone to whom she could turn. Dieter's mother, the Baroness. They had met only once, but Melody had discerned a certain sympathy and liking for her, behind the cool, aristocratic façade that lady presented to the world. She was both resilient and resourceful—she would know what to do.

Buoyed up with new hope, Melody carefully retraced the route they had taken that day. She did not know the actual address, or even the name of the square, and had to be guided by her memory, but it did not fail her. The narrow streets she had walked with Dieter were imprinted faithfully on her mind, and very soon she found herself crossing the square with the fountain, and standing outside the baroque house where the Baroness lived.

A maid showed her into the lounge, where she waited for a few minutes, feeling just a little nervous, and then the Baroness came in, smiling.

'Melody! How sweet of you to visit me,' she said. 'I did so hope we would meet again.'

Then her perceptive glance took in the girl's expression, taut behind her smile, the hurt in the hazel eyes, and the hint of dejection in her stance, and she said, 'But I can see this is not purely a social call. Something is wrong, am I not correct? Do come and sit down, and tell me about it.'

In a low voice, Melody said,

'It's a bit of an impertinence, but I came to you because I did not have anyone else to turn to. I hope you don't mind.'

'Mind? No, indeed, why should I? It is a long time since anyone came to me in need, and I am flattered. But how can I help you?'

'I'm not sure,' Melody said, frowning a little. 'The thing is, Frau Schulz asked me to leave. A girl I knew, back in England, turned up and told her all about a . . . a scandal I was involved in, some time ago, and . . .'

'And Eva dismissed you,' the Baroness finished.

'Yes.' Melody looked her directly in the eyes. 'If you like, I'll tell you exactly what it was all about.'

'You will do no such thing. What happened in the past is your own business,' she said fastidiously. 'I am sure you are not a criminal, and have done nothing to be ashamed of. Furthermore, I have known Eva Schulz since she was virtually a schoolgirl, and I know she can be a little high-handed. I expect she gave you little chance to defend yourself.'

'I tried, but she would not believe me,' Melody said. 'However, if she no longer chooses to employ me, that is her right, and I have to abide by her decision. But you see, I did a very stupid thing. I packed and left in such a hurry that I left all my important documents behind— my cheque book and credit cards, even my passport. I have no money, and no means of withdrawing any, and without my passport I can't go back to England. I'm in such a mess!' she blurted out finally.

'Yes you are, rather, aren't you?' the Baroness agreed, and to Melody's surprise, there was a faintly humorous twinkle in her eyes. 'You poor child, you certainly have had a dreadful day. But don't worry. Since you have had the good sense to come to me, I shall play the fairy godmother and sort out this muddle for you.'

Relief began to flow through Melody's veins.

'You will? Oh, that's wonderful! But how?' she asked curiously.

'Very easily. I shall do a little telephoning . . . later

. . . and arrange for someone to call at the Schulz house and pick up these things for you and bring them to you here. For tonight, you shall stay with me. You see. It is no problem.' She dismissed the entire business with an airy wave of her slender, fine-veined hand.

'It's so very kind of you,' Melody breathed gratefully. 'You know someone who would do that?'

'I know plenty of people,' the Baroness said unconcernedly. 'I do not have any trouble getting a small errand like that done for me. Now—the guest-room is always in readiness, so I shall ask the maid to show you up. I expect you would like a wash before you join me for dinner?'

Words could not have expressed the relief and thankfulness in Melody's heart as she washed and changed in the guest-room. A fairy godmother indeed, she thought, taking in the huge, old-fashioned bed with its vast feather duvet, where she was to spend the night and the cavernous wardrobe in which she hung her navy suit ready for the plane journey tomorrow. There were clean, fluffy towels and delicately scented soap, and from across the square the church clock chimed welcomingly. She did not feel strange in this house, it was almost like coming home. Most likely Dieter stayed here sometimes, perhaps in this same room, she thought, with a sudden tightening of her throat.

They ate dinner, just the two of them, in the dining-room overlooking the small courtyard, and Melody noted that the table was laid with the finest china, crystal glassware, and heavy, solid silver cutlery. There were flowers on the table, and a silver epergne at its centre, and she did not think that any of this finery had been brought out especially in her honour.

'One has to maintain a certain style,' the Baroness

said dryly, following her gaze. 'Because one is getting old, and lives alone, that is no excuse for sloppiness and falling standards, don't you agree?'

'I think if you have nice things, it is as well to use them, rather than shut them away in cupboards,' Melody agreed. Behind her hostess' cool and elegant exterior, dwelt a warm and sympathetic personality she realised, and if its owner was careful most of the time not to reveal it too readily, it was nonetheless there.

'Precisely. Would you care to pour some more wine, my dear.'

Melody poured carefully into the crystal glasses, and the Baroness said, 'I tell myself that I am only the custodian of all these refinements I have inherited or collected, and that they will be Dieter's one day, and through him remain in the family. I hope, when the time comes for that to happen, he will have a real home to give them, not simply a room where he works and occasionally sleeps, and plays endless music on his far too expensive stereo equipment.'

'I imagine his way of life will change when he is married,' Melody replied carefully.

'I hope so,' the other said, fervently. 'It is my dearest wish to see him happily married, but of course, a mature man does not discuss such matters with his mother! Naturally, I am aware that there have been a number of women in his life. There was a soprano from the opera house, I seem to recall, and a young woman doctor he was friendly with when he lived in America. But they were only diversions.'

And naturally, Melody thought, the Baroness would accept that her son had known a variety of other women, whilst waiting for the girl he had chosen to reach maturity. No one would find anything exceptionable in that, any more than they would object to the droves of young men like Klaus Becker, who had flocked around Kristina before her accident. Merely amusements, not intended to detract from the mainstream of their lives, which would be lived together. She remembered Kristina once saying the Baroness approved of her as a future daughter-in-law, and could not resist asking,

'Would you have minded . . . if he had married the singer from the opera house?'

'Not if she had been the one he wanted,' she replied, 'and I was sure she was marrying him for the right reasons, not simply because he is professionally successful and has a title to inherit—which, incidentally, he never even cares to use. I am not a snob, my dear, and Dieter is even less so.'

She looked closely at Melody, who took refuge in an intent study of the tablecloth, not wishing to betray her own interest in Dieter's affairs. By this time tomorrow she would be far away, involved no longer in these people's lives. She was merely an outsider, who had briefly disturbed the calm surface of their existence.

The day which had begun with such deceptive normality had turned out to be eventful in the extreme. Melody was truly exhausted, and fell asleep the moment she sank gratefully into the vast *federbed*. She slept late, too, and was only awakened by the arrival of the maid who brought her breakfast in bed, along with the Baroness' insistence that she take as much time as she wanted.

Melody could not remember a time when she had indulged in this unashamed leisure. Back in England, she was usually up early to go on duty, and even on her days off or late duty days, the constant comings and goings along the corridors of the nurses' home had made

staying in bed no pleasure. And recently she had always
been up early to attend to Kristina's breakfast tray. But
to sit up in this enormous bed, with pillows supporting
her back, and a small table across her knees laid with
coffee, rolls and jam, all on a crisp lace cloth, was a rare
indulgence. She would not easily forget the kindness of
Dieter's mother, a lady as gracious as the city she called
home.

But she did not linger for long in this unaccustomed
laziness. She got up, bathed and put on her suit, and
made sure everything was packed away in her suitcase
before going downstairs. There she found the Baroness
looking sprightly and extremely pleased with herself.

'Your business is all taken care of,' she told Melody.
'Let us go for a short stroll in the sunshine. It is pleasant
for me to have a companion of your age, and I must
make the most of it. When we come back it will be time
for lunch, and by then, your passport should have
arrived.'

But lunch was eaten and cleared away, and there was
still no sign of the Baroness' messenger. She seemed
slightly agitated, and Melody noted that she kept glancing at the clock, and listening with great attention to the
chimes from the church opposite the apartment.

'Please don't worry,' Melody said. 'There is plenty of
time before the plane leaves, and it will not take me long
to get to the airport. I'm so sorry to have inconvenienced
you.'

'You have not inconvenienced me at all. I am merely
concerned that the arrangements I have made are satis-
factorily concluded. Once you have your passport you
must not feel you then have to rush off and jump on the
first plane. Stay as long as you wish.'

'You are very generous, but I really think I should

leave,' Melody said quietly. 'I've caused enough trouble of one kind or another.'

'The only trouble people like you cause is for themselves,' the Baroness said emphatically.

The discreet ring of the doorbell prevented Melody from inquiring more closely into the meaning of this. Instead of allowing the maid to answer it, the Baroness got up and went briskly to the door herself.

'I wonder what kept you so long!' Melody heard her exclaim. 'You certainly took your time!'

'Since it was I who had to venture into the lion's den, and then extricate myself once more, I don't feel you should complain too much,' said a dry, amused and affectionate voice that caused Melody to leap from her Louis XIV chair with alacrity, the roof of her mouth suddenly dry, and her heart reverberating so she felt her lungs would burst.

'Dieter!' she gasped, as his tall frame followed the slight, spry figure of his mother into the room.

'Yes, indeed,' he said. 'Who else would my mother telephone at dead of night to do an errand such as this for her?'

He smiled, a reserved, indrawn smile that revealed nothing of how he really felt about being entrusted with this mission.

'I have your passport and cheque book, Melody, obtained at risk of life and limb. Eva is in a distinctly warlike mood this morning, since she has discovered that you are not, as she had imagined, safely back in England.'

Melody, still not recovered from the shock of his arrival, said shakily, 'I'm sorry to have involved you in any unpleasantness.'

'Don't apologise to him. Can't you see he's only

teasing the pair of us?' the Baroness said, her eyes
sparkling with humour. Melody looked from one to the
other of them, sensing a conspiracy, sure that it was no
oversight that she had not been informed exactly who
would be bringing her passport.

'I thought you were still in America,' she said lamely.

'I arrived home yesterday,' he said, 'as my mother
knew, since I sent her a telegram to that effect before I
left the States.'

'I'm grateful to you,' she said stiffly. 'I'm sure you
must be very tired after such a long flight. It was good of
you to go to so much trouble on my account. If you'll
give me my passport, I'll be on my way.'

'Oddly enough, I am not tired at all,' he contradicted.
'The car is outside. I'll drive you.'

'There's really . . .' she began, but he cut short her
protest.

'I know. There's no need, I don't have to, and I must
not feel obliged,' he said, and his smile, now, was the
gentle one she knew so well, which concealed the iron
strength of character behind it. 'I'm well acquainted with
all your objections, Melody. Nevertheless, please get
into the car.'

The Baroness gave her a brief kiss on the cheek.

'Go on, child,' she urged. 'Arguing with him is pointless—and I should know.'

Melody gave in.

'Very well. Goodbye, and thank you for everything,'
she said gratefully.

'It was nothing. And we don't say "goodbye" here, we
say "*auf Wiedersehen*!' the Baroness said with a smile.
'Until we see each other again.'

Seated for the first time in the front seat of his car,
Melody did not speak as they nosed their way through

the narrow streets leading out of the now crowded city. Only when they emerged on to the open road, and she felt the need to break the silence, did she manage to ask politely, 'How was the conference?'

'Extremely verbose,' he replied laconically. 'It is in their nature to be so, of course, but this one was more long-winded than usual, or at least, so it seemed to me. Perhaps I was anxious to be back. And as it happened, it is a good job I arrived home when I did.'

'Did you . . . did you see Kristina this morning?' she asked nervously.

'No. She was still in her room. I was monopolised by Eva, who was determined to give me a run down on your transgressions, until I ended up with a few hard words of my own,' he said grimly.

'Oh, Dieter, you shouldn't have made things unpleasant for yourself on my account,' she said wretchedly.

'No matter. It's high time someone talked straight to Eva. No one does, not even Hugo, who is still not convinced she cares for him as she did for that Englishman she was married to before,' he said. 'You are not a very good advocate in your own defence, Melody, so someone has to do it for you.'

She could not bring herself to look at him. Not fifteen minutes ago, she had imagined him to be three thousand miles away across the Atlantic, and now she was sitting beside him. The unexpectedness of it was too much, and she did not know whether she wished this short drive to the airport to be over as soon as possible or to go on for ever. There was nothing to be gained by his coming but the sweet, awful agony of prolonging the farewell. It would have been better not to have seen him again, she told herself, and wished she could believe it.

They passed one of the signs marked '*Flughafen*' and a little further on, yet another. Melody sat upright, and now she did turn her head towards him.

'Dieter? You've just missed the turning for the airport.'

'I know,' he replied tranquilly.

'But I shall miss my flight!' she pointed out, in some agitation.

'There will be other flights. Relax, Melody. You are not going to the airport, and since I have your passport in my pocket and we're travelling at approximately fifty miles per hour there's very little you can do about it.'

She gasped. His face, in profile, seemed perfectly composed, he was smiling a little, but apparently concentrating on the road ahead.

'Then where are we going?' she demanded.

'I suggest you wait and see,' he said mysteriously. 'You are forever wanting to escape from me, but this time I am not going to stand by and let you do it.'

Her hazel eyes opened very wide.

'Take me to the airport—please!' she insisted. 'You can't abduct me like this!'

'You are being a little melodramatic,' he said mildly. 'Can you not spare me a few hours of your time, which might make a difference to your life?'

Melody fell silent. Beneath her agitation, she was aware of a delicious excitement as she savoured the knowledge that he was right, and there was absolutely nothing she could do to prevent him from taking her any place he chose. Maybe it was wrong, but her heart had begun to beat wildly and she wondered how they were going to spend those few hours. Could it be that he wanted her, and was not going to let her leave without bringing to a head the suppressed attraction that had flared between them from the start? Whilst part of her indignantly insisted that she was not to be used and disposed of in so cavalier a fashion, another part was recklessly saying yes.

She stopped romanticising that she was being spirited away like some captive princess about to be seduced, when the road began to look alarmingly familiar.

'I am *not* going back to the Schulz place,' she said firmly. 'Anything but that!'

'Anything?' he replied, raising amused eyebrows. 'Don't worry, Melody. I don't imagine either of us would be too welcome there today.'

With relief she noted that where the road forked, they took the other turning, and very soon she recognised the route they had taken the day she had visited Heiligen-kreuz. She remained silent as they retraced that journey. The suspicion which had lurked in her mind earlier was unworthy of her, she decided. He had not had seduction in mind at all, but was reintroducing the idea of her coming to work for him. What motivated him was pity for a lonely girl he had caused to fall in love with him, and a desire to do the decent thing, rather than leave her alone and without support in a harsh world.

There was an acid taste in her mouth, and a sensation that the world had turned to ashes. She wished that her fantasy had been the truth, that she could have been his captive princess for a few hours, after all.

He drew the car to a halt outside the hospital and opened the door for her to get out, but he did not take her into the main building, as he had on her previous visit.

'You've seen all that. Come and see where I live,' he said, and she followed him mechanically along a path flanked by flowering shrubs.

What the Baroness had distastefully called 'a room
where he works, and sleeps occasionally' turned out, in
fact, to be a small, modern bungalow, screened from the
hospital complex by mature trees. But entering it, she
knew what that lady had meant. Everything was clean,
comfortable, functional, but it was in no sense a home.
Dieter did not 'live' here, in the true sense of the word.
He 'lived' in the hospital. This was merely where he
spent his off-duty hours. A small study, its desk littered
with papers, was the only room that showed clear
evidence of his occupation. The living-room into
which he showed Melody was immaculate and undisturbed.

He went into the kitchen, and returned carrying a
bottle of wine. Melody was standing by the window, and
as he extracted the cork and poured the sparkling liquid
into two tall, fluted glasses, he said,

'The entire complex was designed by our mutual
friend, Hugo Schulz, and there you have his hallmark,
his architectural signature, so to speak, the sheer wall of
glass, bringing the exterior right into the house. He's
known for it.'

'With exteriors like you have here in Austria, who
could blame him?' Melody said, accepting her drink, but
eyeing her companion warily. 'Even here, the hospital
might be miles away, one is aware of nothing but hills
and trees.'

'Indeed,' he acquiesced, and met the question in the
hazel eyes upturned to his. 'You are wondering why I
brought you here, aren't you? My ancestors in the
sixteenth century were in business as robber barons, but
it seems strange virtually to kidnap a girl and carry her
off to a psychiatric hospital, of all places.'

'I had not imagined you brought me here to play

Rapunzel,' she said tersely. 'To offer me a job, perhaps?'

He lifted a strand of her hair between his fingers, and let it fall again.

'Rapunzel was blonde, I believe, and you are burnished chestnut,' he said. 'And if by offering you a job, you think I intend employing you as a nurse—well, I made that suggestion to you once, but it was not in my mind to do so today. Neither did I intend to take you by storm, so you can stop looking at me with such apprehension. I meant only to buy us a little time, so we might finally settle what is between us.'

'There is nothing between us,' she said, with a decisiveness she was far from feeling. 'Why, if you had come back from America a day later, I would have been gone, and you would never have seen me again. Can't you just take me to the airport, and let us behave as if it had happened that way?'

'No, we cannot,' he replied, with equal firmness. 'It isn't really an answer. Do you think England is so far away I should not have found you, had I chosen to?' He set down his glass and put both hands on her slim shoulders, looking down into her face. 'I believe that you love me, Melody, for all you keep holding back and running away. Tell me I'm mistaken, and we shall get into the car this very minute and drive to the airport. Only first, look me in the eyes and say "I do not love you".'

'That's unfair!' she said, in a small voice, and he said, 'I know, but this is too important to be played by the rules. A girl like you does not kiss a man she does not love the way you kissed me. Like this, Melody.'

He took the glass from her hand and set it down, and as he drew her purposefully into his arms, she felt her resistance ebbing dangerously away, a weak, pointless thing, helpless against the force of her love for him.

'*Ich liebe dich*, Melody. I love you,' he said between kisses, and she clung to him, unable to believe what she was hearing.

'You love *me*?' she said incredulously, as he released her a little, still keeping a firm grip on the small hands enclosed in his. 'I thought I was merely a diversion . . . that you were amusing yourself.'

'I thought so too, at first,' he admitted, 'although I was drawn to you, somewhat reluctantly, from the time we sat together on the plane. But it soon became clear to me that this was something more, something for which I had waited a long time. I want to marry you, Melody. You are the other half of me, without which I shall always be incomplete, and I want you in my life always.'

'But we can't!' she said, tears coming to her eyes. 'I love you too, but it would be wrong for me to take my happiness at Kristina's expense. You must have loved her once, before the accident.'

He frowned a little.

'Kristina has been dear to me since she was a child, but I have never loved her,' he said, with quiet emphasis.

'But you are engaged to marry her—albeit unofficially,' Melody protested.

He kept hold of her hands, but made no attempt to draw her back into his arms. His voice was calm, but somehow dangerous, as he said,

'I wish you would tell me how long you have been labouring under that misapprehension, and who led you to believe it in the first place?'

Melody looked up at him with puzzled, innocent eyes.

'Why, Kristina did, of course! She told me so the very first day I met her, after you had been to dinner. And

later, Frau Schulz told me more or less the same thing—
that there had been an understanding to that effect for
years. Kristina said that even your mother knew and had
given her approval.'

He gave a shout of derisive laughter.

'My mother!' he said incredulously. 'Can you honestly
imagine her agreeing to anything like that, on my be-
half? Now that I come to think of it, I believe that once,
years ago, Eva mentioned to her that it would be nice if
Kristina and I were to discover an attachment for each
other. My mother, in her inimitable manner, said something to the effect that it was entirely up to us, and if Eva
chose to interpret that as approval, she was jumping
the gun! I expect Mother promptly forgot about it, and
never gave it another thought. We don't arrange
things that way, nowadays, any more than you do in
England.'

Melody, still reeling with the implications of what he
had said, with the wonderful knowledge that he was free
to love her, nevertheless knew she had to clarify the
situation.

'Kristina is very serious about this, Dieter. She be-
lieves you are going to marry her.'

He said, 'Now let us get this straight. Kristina has had
an infatuation for me since she was very young, and I
would have been a fool not to know it, but if this accident
had not happened she would have outgrown it, in time.
As it is, it has become something of a fixation. To a
certain extent I have gone along with her possessiveness,
in order not to increase her mental instability, which was
not difficult whilst there was no special woman in my life.
That was the reason I played down, and initially tried to
suppress, my feelings for you. I have great sympathy for
Kristina, and up to a point I feel responsible for her, and

always will. I shall continue to be her caring and support-ive *friend*.

'But I swear to you, Melody, there was never an engagement, or any understanding to which I was a party. She and Eva must have dreamed that up between them. Kristina was deluding herself, which in her con-dition one can perhaps excuse, and Eva was very wrong to have encouraged her.'

Melody said, 'Oh Dieter, and all this time, even though I loved you, I dared not give way to my feelings because of Kristina.'

'You have too stern a conscience, my love,' he told her with a smile. 'An admirable quality, in many ways, but let me tell you this. If you and I had never met, I would not have married Kristina Schulz. Should you walk out on me, today—which I don't intend letting you do—still, I should not marry her. It would be disastrous, for both parties. Kristina has a lot of growing up still to do, and there may be many men before she finally meets the right one. She has first to discover herself. I would be totally wrong for her. My work is such a vital part of my life, and yet it is something which she could not begin to accept and understand.'

His assurance, so definite and unequivocal, dispelled the shadows which had stood for so long between Melody and her heart's need. And all those other shad-ows in her past seemed to fade too. Maybe they would never leave her entirely, but with his love and his strength to support her in all she did, she knew she need no longer fear that they would overwhelm her again.

'Shall I tell you when I first began to realise that I loved you?' he said. 'It was that afternoon when I called and found you alone, you remember? You made tea for us. And then you said you wished you could play the piano. It seemed such a simple thing, and yet you had lacked the opportunity. I wanted to take you away from your loneliness and insecurity and give you all the things you had never had—music, travel, a home of your own, a family. I wanted to open up the world for you.'

'And you have, my love,' Melody said happily. 'But it only took your love to do that. Please kiss me again, and then I can be sure that this is really happening.'

'If that is all the assurance you need, then I am only too willing to provide it,' he said.

The light had begun to fade slowly from the summer sky, and the bubbles to disappear from the wine. But neither of them noticed, or cared.

CHAPTER TWELVE

THEY were married on a summer day, at the small church across the square from where the Baroness lived. Very quietly, since that same afternoon they were to fly to Australia to attend a conference, so their only celebration was a special lunch provided by Dieter's mother.

'When you come back, I shall throw a splendid party for you,' she insisted. 'All Salzburg must come to meet my new daughter-in-law, and I shall tell them how I knew, before either of the people concerned, that they would marry. Yes I did, Dieter, don't protest. Not that you told me in so many words, but from the way you spoke of this Melody, whom I had not met, I knew that she must have the elusive quality you had been seeking for so many years.'

'I'll allow you your burst of clairvoyance, Mother,' he said fondly. 'As for the party for all Salzburg, I don't know where you will fit them all in.' He glanced round the small, elegant room. 'Perhaps we should hire the Hohensalzburg?'

'Will you be inviting the Schulzes?' Melody asked, a little nervously, and the Baroness flashed her a reassuring smile.

'Perhaps not. It will take Eva a little while to accept that my son was not her daughter's predestined husband,' she said. 'In any event, they will most likely still be in Antibes, so we shall be spared the decision.'

Melody returned her smile. She could not find it in her to nurture any hard feelings towards Eva for the way she

184

had behaved to her. Although misguided, she had had her daughter's interests at heart, and this fierce maternal devotion had blinded her to the harsh fact that it was not always possible to make others fall into line with what one had planned. And as Melody now had all she ever wanted, and more than she had dreamed of, she could afford to be magnanimous.

She had not seen Eva since that fateful day she had walked out of her house in disgrace, but whilst she was staying with the Baroness pending her marriage, a note had come to her from Kristina:

> Melody—don't just run off and get married without even seeing me. Come up to the house on Saturday morning—please. I promise Mutti will be out.
>
> Kristina.

She had used the word 'please' which was unusual for Kristina, and Melody did not feel able to refuse this request, although she set out with some trepidation, not quite sure of what kind of reception awaited her.

But she was greeted in the hall by Hugo, and his warm smile of greeting and hearty congratulations assured her that he had had no part in the scheming of his women-folk. Max was there, too, eager to show her the new model aeroplane he had made, and Siegfried slobbered expansively all over her. Even Lindi waved and smiled shyly from the kitchen door. Melody felt strangely touched by their welcome.

'So you came.'

She turned, to be confronted by a sight she had once despaired of ever seeing. Kristina, *standing* in the door-way of the lounge, supporting herself on crutches. The golden eyes were slightly shadowed with pain, but there was a glimmer of a smile touching her lips.

'Did you think that I wouldn't?' Melody challenged.

'Not really,' Kristina acknowledged. 'You're too conscientious to refuse, even though, strictly speaking, I'm no longer your concern. Come into the lounge where we can talk undisturbed.'

She shot a meaningful glance at her brother as she said this, and he grinned.

'I get the message. Girl chat. Come on, Siegfried, let's go for a walk.'

Kristina lowered herself carefully into a chair, after traversing the room slowly, but under her own steam, declining Melody's assistance.

'No thanks, I can manage. I have to, as you told me—remember? You said it would hurt, too, and you were right. It does.'

'To begin with. It will become gradually easier.'

'It had better, that's all I can say.' Kristina looked directly at Melody. 'I once said to you that all was fair in love and war. There's another saying—may the best man, or woman, win. And I suppose she did.'

The tone was not accusing, but light and deliberately free of reproach, but Melody was too sensitive not to catch the note of underlying pain.

'It wasn't like that, Kristina,' she said quietly. 'I never set out to take Dieter from you. It was just something that *happened*, something we could not prevent happening.'

'Do you think I don't know that?' the other girl said, 'or that it makes it any easier? I could see from the start how it was. He was always kind to me, always affectionate, but he treated me like some kind of kid cousin. You, he looked at and spoke to as a man does to a woman, on equal terms. I tried to pretend otherwise, to myself and to you. *Mutti* tried, too. But it wasn't any use, was it?'

'I'm sorry,' was all Melody could say.

'Don't be. I shouldn't, in your place. It isn't possible to take from someone that which they have only deluded themselves into believing was theirs. Dieter came to see me, did you know?'

Melody knew. In the interest of Kristina's recovery, she had finally, after much insistent prompting from him, told him the full story of what had taken place on her last day there, how the girl had been impelled to make an attempt to walk, and how she had confessed the reason for her erstwhile refusal to do so.

'But she must never know I told you this,' Melody had begged him. 'She would die of humiliation.' He had told her, simply, to leave it to him, and she knew and accepted that as long as they lived, he would feel this kind of care and concern for Kristina.

'He was very kind, as always, very tactful,' Kristina told her, now. 'He must know how I felt about him, but not for an instant did he let on. He spared me that. He told me you and he were to be married, and he knew I'd be happy for you both, but he didn't labour the point. Then we just chatted, generally, about the course I'm planning to take next term. I expect he knew he'd have to be ruthless and pull the props from beneath me, so I didn't go on cherishing false hopes, but it was all done as painlessly a possible.'

She grimaced.

'So I'm on my feet—finally. I hope you're satisfied now.'

'I wish I could make you understand how glad I am,' Melody said. 'You don't see it now, because you're hurting, in more ways than one, but you're young and good looking and talented. Everything's in front of you.'

Kristina shrugged.

'I expect you're right,' she acquiesced grandly. 'Anyhow, we're off to Antibes for the summer—*Mutti* has friends there—so I shan't be around on your big day. I shall be stretched out on the beach, luring the local talent with my charms, with my crutches carefully hidden beneath a towel.'

Melody had to smile. Kristina was acquiring a new wisdom and maturity, beneath her flippant manner, and she had guts. The girl would make it, she believed. It was too soon, yet, but one day, she hoped they would be able to be friends.

'You had better go, now, before *Mutti* gets back,' Kristina warned her briskly. 'She's not quite ready to let bygones be bygones just yet. Anyway, I expect you are busy, house-hunting, and so on.'

Melody gave a mock groan.

'We've looked at more houses than you've had hot dinners! Dieter says we can't possibly start married life in his bungalow at the hospital, although I'd be quite happy to do so. I'd live anywhere, so long as I'm with him.'

Kristina favoured her with a strange look.

'I believe you would,' she said. 'I find it hard to understand.'

'When you really fall in love, you will,' Melody promised her. As she drove away, the last she saw of Kristina was her hand raised in a jaunty, defiant salute as she stood by the window.

The wedding lunch was finished, and they sat for a long time over their coffee, but finally, Dieter looked at his watch.

'Well come along, Baroness, I hate to rush you, but we do have a plane to catch,' he said, and as Melody started, he said, with a laugh, 'Yes, *you*, *liebchen*. Does it surprise you to hear yourself addressed in that way?'

'Please,' she said breathlessly, 'allow me a little time to get used to being Frau von Rheinhof, first!'

'All the time in the world,' he said, and taking his wife's hand firmly in his, he led her out to the waiting car. Once again, she would be flying with him into the blue, but this time his ring was on her finger, and today, and for the rest of their lives, they would be together.

Doctor Nurse Romances

Amongst the intense emotional pressures of modern medical life, doctors and nurses often find romance. Read about their lives and loves in the other three Doctor Nurse titles available this month.

SECOND CHANCE AT LOVE
by Zara Holman

Sister Hana Dean had left her post at a London teaching hospital because of an unhappy love affair. So when she clashes with surgeon Jake Carlyon at the Bridgestead Cottage Hospital can her self-respect allow him to drive her back?

CASSANDRA BY CHANCE
by Betty Neels

Benedict van Manfeld, a brilliant surgeon whose sight had been severely damaged in an accident, has some excuse for his ill-temper. But is that the only reason Nurse Cassandra Darling continues to put up with his ranting and raging?

TRIO OF DOCTORS
by Lindsay Hicks

'I never fall in love with nurses. They can be more dangerous than female patients.'
So Mark Barlow coolly informs Nurse Gillian Grant at their turbulent first encounter. But Gillian is in no danger of falling for the arrogant surgeon — or is she?

Mills & Boon
the rose of romance